FLIES

#1 Secre

#2 Mystery

#3 Th

#

#5 F

#6 T

#7 S

#

#9 Th

#

#12

AS THE FALCON

MYSTERIES IN THE
YS ADVENTURES:

et of the Red Arrow
 of the Phantom Heist
ne Vanishing Game
4 Into Thin Air
Peril at Granite Peak
The Battle of Bayport
hadows at Predator Reef
8 Deception on the Set
e Curse of the Ancient Emerald
#10 Tunnel of Secrets
11 Shuwdown at Widow Creek
The Madman of Black Bear Mountain
#13 Bound for Danger
#14 Attack of the Bayport Beast
#15 A Con Artist in Paris
#16 Stolen Identity
#17 The Gray Hunter's Revenge
#18 The Disappearance
#19 Dungeons & Detectives
#20 Return to Black Bear Mountain
#21 A Treacherous Tide
#22 Trouble Island
#23 Mystery on the Mayhem Express

COMING SOON:
#25 The Smuggler's Legacy

HARDY BOYS
ADVENTURES™

#24 *AS THE FALCON FLIES*

FRANKLIN W. DIXON

ALADDIN   New York London Toronto Sydney New Delhi

ALADDIN
An imprint of Simon & Schuster Children's Publishing Division
1230 Avenue of the Americas, New York, New York 10020
First Aladdin hardcover edition January 2022
Text copyright © 2022 by Simon & Schuster, Inc.
Jacket illustration copyright © 2022 by Kevin Keele
THE HARDY BOYS MYSTERY SERIES, HARDY BOYS ADVENTURES, and related logos are trademarks of Simon & Schuster, Inc.
Also available in an Aladdin paperback edition.

ALADDIN and related logo are registered trademarks of Simon & Schuster, Inc.
For information about special discounts for bulk purchases, please contact Simon & Schuster Special Sales at 1-866-506-1949 or business@simonandschuster.com.
The Simon & Schuster Speakers Bureau can bring authors to your live event. For more information or to book an event contact the Simon & Schuster Speakers Bureau at 1-866-248-3049 or visit our website at www.simonspeakers.com.
Series designed by Karin Paprocki
Jacket designed by Tiara Iandiorio and Ginny Kemmerer
Interior designed by Mike Rosamilia
The text of this book was set in Adobe Carlson Pro.
Manufactured in the United States of America 1121 FFG
2 4 6 8 10 9 7 5 3 1
Library of Congress Cataloging-in-Publication Data
Names: Dixon, Franklin W., author.
Title: As the Falcon Flies / by Franklin W. Dixon.
Description: New York : Aladdin, [2022] | Series: Hardy Boys adventures; 24 |
Audience: Ages 8 to 12. | Summary: During their Alaskan vacation, Frank and Joe Hardy help falconer Kate when her beloved peregrine goes missing.
Identifiers: LCCN 2021032186 (print) | LCCN 2021032187 (ebook) |
ISBN 9781534483255 (paperback) | ISBN 9781534483262 (hardcover) |
ISBN 9781534483279 (ebook)
Subjects: CYAC: Mystery and detective stories. | Alaska—Fiction. | Peregrine falcon—Fiction. |
Falcons—Fiction. | Lost and found possessions—Fiction. | Brothers—Fiction.
Classification: LCC PZ7.D644 As 2022 (print) | LCC PZ7.D644 (ebook) | DDC [Fic]—dc23
LC record available at https://lccn.loc.gov/2021032186
LC ebook record available at https://lccn.loc.gov/2021032187

CONTENTS

Chapter 1   Headed North   1

Chapter 2   Rules of Flight   12

Chapter 3   Gone   22

Chapter 4   The Hunt Begins   27

Chapter 5   Interrogation   37

Chapter 6   A Dead End   44

Chapter 7   A Midnight Meeting   54

Chapter 8   Following Footprints   59

Chapter 9   Fireside Deceptions   69

Chapter 10   A New Lead   81

Chapter 11   Hot on the Trail   89

Chapter 12   The Dinner Party   98

Chapter 13   Out of Time   108

Chapter 14   The Showdown   118

Chapter 15   Heading Home   127

HEADED NORTH

1

JOE

ET'S JUST GET ONE THING STRAIGHT. I do *not* have a fear of heights. Frank had been looking at me out of the corner of his eye, going totally older brother on me the whole flight because my knuckles had been white on the armrests since we took off, but what did he expect? It was windy! There was ocean everywhere! And a ton of the flight involved going over Canada, which meant if we went down, it was straight into the wilderness. I didn't think being a little nervous was unreasonable.

The second we landed, I jumped up, nearly hitting my head on the luggage compartment above us.

"Settle down, Joe," said Frank.

"You settle down!"

My heart was pounding in my chest, *not* because I was afraid of heights, remember. Just because I was a guy who liked to take precautions.

Or something.

I glanced out the window at the airfield, reminding myself that we were flat on the ground, and exhaled. "Sorry," I mumbled.

"It's okay," said my brother. He looked completely fine—I mean, utterly unconcerned by totally possible risks.

We waited in the plane for what felt like forever, until finally, it was time for those of us near the back to deplane. Frank and I got our bags and shuffled through the little aisle. I about thwacked an old lady in the face with my duffel bag and had to double back to make sure she was all right.

She was. I hadn't clipped her, *thankfully.*

Frank strode ahead of me on the jetway, and we waited for our parents to meet us, then together made our way into the Anchorage, Alaska, airport.

It was . . . small. Not that crowded. Nothing like the airports back east.

"Whoa," I said. "Would you look at that?"

Inside a huge plexiglass case in front of us was the biggest bear I had ever seen. He was taxidermized, brown and bushy, standing on his hind legs, his massive paws and Wolverine-style claws out, frozen mid-roar.

"You know," said Dad, coming up behind us and about

making me jump out of my skin, "that bear's the biggest grizzly ever taken in the United States."

"Really?" said Frank.

"Yup. I read up on it last time we came through. They say when he was found, he had the remains of two people in his belly. . . ."

"A man-eater," I whispered reverently. Suddenly the bear seemed even bigger and the plexiglass case felt thinner. It wasn't fear I was feeling—not exactly. Just awe.

Not my usual reaction in an airport, unless there's a Caribou Coffee selling pastries near the gate.

"You know that's a tall tale as well as I do, Fenton Hardy."

We all turned around to find Ed Adenshaw behind us, smiling big and wide. My dad's face split nearly in half with the force of his matching grin, and my mom started to bounce on her feet. Frank and I had known the Adenshaws and their daughter since we were little, and our parents had known them a lot longer than that. Mom and Ed's wife, Jacqueline, had gone to school together. The rest was history, or so they liked to remind us every time they were together—which wasn't often. Alaska and Bayport weren't exactly close together. Ed had always seemed a little larger than life to us as kids, mostly because he was. He told stories like no one else did, and laughed longer, ate more, sang louder, and danced harder. He did everything *big*. He was broad-shouldered and had short, sharply cut black hair, bronzed skin, and eyes that crinkled when he smiled. He didn't look as tall now as he had when I was four years old and they'd come to see us, but even so, he had an energy about him that made me want to stand a little straighter, be a little more impressive, too.

"A tall tale?" Dad replied. "No way."

"Sure it is. That bear is two hundred pounds under the record for a taken grizzly."

"And its supposed victims?" asked Frank, eyeing the bear warily.

"Not true." Ed hoisted one of my mom's bags up on one of his shoulders and one of my dad's on the other. "Grizzlies look big and bad, but all those teeth and claws are for eating berries and fish. Maybe human garbage, if they can get to it. But almost never people, not unless they're starving. That guy look like he was starving to you?"

He did not.

"I knew it," I said. "I knew there weren't man-eating bears in Alaska."

Ed gave me a wink. "I didn't say *that*."

I raised my eyebrows at Frank, and we made our way out of the airport.

This was going to be one wild spring break.

The parents chatted the whole way to the Adenshaws' place, which left Frank and me to talk in the back seat of the truck. Or we would have if Frank didn't have his face buried in his phone. "No work this week," I said. "Remember?"

"I'm not working!" Frank protested. "I'm—"

"Texting your girlfriend."

"She's not my girlfriend, Joe. She's just, well, someone I like."

"Uh-huh." Ever since Frank had summoned up the courage to ask Charlene Vale, reporter for the *Bayport High News*, to the movies, they'd been going nonstop—texting, talking on the phone, liking each other's stuff on social media, hanging out. They sure seemed like an item to me. I'd been looking forward to having Frank all to myself this week. We could just be us again, have some real brotherly bonding time.

It was going to be strange not having any cases to solve, though. Before we left Bayport, we'd promised our parents. We were on vacation to a place I could barely remember; I'd been so little last time we came. This week was for friends, family, and enjoying Alaska.

From what I'd already seen, it was pretty gorgeous—mountains jutting up into the ice-blue skyline, water everywhere, air so clear that just breathing it didn't feel like enough. I wanted to *drink* it.

"What's the first thing you wanna do while we're here?" Frank asked.

I shrugged. "Check out a tide pool? Do the polar bear plunge?"

Frank snorted. "It's not the right time of year for the polar bear plunge."

"Still. That water's gotta be cold."

"Fair enough."

Mom had told us about the charity event where a bunch of people go splashing around in the ocean in the middle of winter when the water's at its coldest. It sounded completely bananas.

I was so in.

I was still thinking about how much the ice-cold water would hurt when we rolled up the old paved road to the Adenshaws' place. Their house sat on a rocky coast, framed by moody clouds and the ocean in the background. The white scalloping, wood, and flowers reminded me of a little gingerbread house.

Dad whistled. "Nice new place you got here, Ed."

"Thanks."

The house I remembered visiting was on the Adenshaws' ancestral land in Sitka, Alaska, which was a few hours to the southeast and a heck of a lot warmer. They'd moved up here to Anchorage a few years ago. Job stuff.

"You liking it here?" Dad asked.

Ed shrugged. "Yeah. It's been good so far. Jacqueline's still not over having to move off Tlingit land. But when opportunity knocks . . ."

The Adenshaws were Tlingit (Jacqueline) and Haida (Ed), and I remembered Mom and Dad talking about the move here being a little tough for them. Especially because their old place had been in Jacqueline's family for years. I think her sister lived there now. Or her brother, maybe? Anyway, this new place was amazing, right on the water. It looked like they had a bunch of land, too. An old wood fence ran two posts up from the ground, bordering their property, and it went so far back into the trees that it disappeared. It looked like we weren't going to need a mystery while we were up here to stumble into an adventure.

When we pulled up to the house and jumped out, the cool salt air hit me right away. It didn't quite smell like it did back home.

I hugged my jacket around me and tried not to look like I was freezing. Sure, it was Alaska, but it was *April.*

Ed pushed through the front door, and Jacqueline and my mom flung themselves at each other. It had been years. Frank walked right up to Jacqueline and held his hand out to shake hers, but I hung back a little. It was always kind of embarrassing meeting adults who'd known you when you were young enough that they might have changed your diapers. Jacqueline looked between Frank and me. "My gosh, I can't believe how big you've both gotten."

I smiled. "Hi, Mrs. Adenshaw."

Then she and Ed waved us into the house.

It was super homey—blankets everywhere, amazing Native art on the walls alongside family pictures, and books all over the place. I wondered which member of the family was the big reader. Maybe all of them. There was a fire going in the stone fireplace in the living room, even in April!

"You all remember our daughter Kate," Jacqueline said.

"Of course," Mom replied, stepping forward to wrap the girl who'd come out to greet us in a hug. Dad joined in, and they did the same adult cooing Kate's parents had done about Frank and me.

I remembered Kate from the last time our families had gotten together. She was around the same age as me and had been kind of gangly, with short, straight black hair and a couple of teeth that hadn't grown in right and—

"Hey," she said, tipping her chin up at us.

Frank flashed her a big smile. "Kate! Wow, last time we saw each other, I'm pretty sure you were in a crayon-eating phase."

"And you were into picking your nose."

He sputtered. "Well, we all grow."

She raised her eyebrow. "Speak for yourself."

Frank scratched his head. "Come again?"

"I'm just saying, do you see any Crayolas around here?"

Frank chuckled, and soon enough, her parents joined in. And then *my* parents were laughing. But I wasn't.

I couldn't.

I just stood there like a fish, my mouth hanging open, heart beating all the way up in my throat.

Kate's hair wasn't short anymore. It fell all the way down to her waist. And her teeth fit her mouth just fine. She had dimples, and . . . *whoa*. I blinked.

I was starting to sound like Frank.

Kate looked at me. "And you. Do you talk?"

"W-what?" I stuttered. "Uh . . ."

The awkward silence was unbearable. I could feel it on my skin. But I had no idea how to break it. Thankfully, just when I was sure I'd bolt from the room rather than embarrass myself any more, Frank elbowed me in the ribs and broke the spell. *What am I doing? I can talk to a girl.*

"Uh, right," I managed to get out. "No."

"You don't . . . talk?" Kate said slowly.

"I mean, yes. I do." Maybe I should have bolted when I had the chance.

Kate looked at Frank, who just shrugged, then back at me. I stood there staring at my toes, hoping I'd sink down beneath the floorboards.

"Well, that settles that, I guess," she said.

"Sure," Frank replied, eyebrow arched.

Kate took a couple of steps toward us, and sweat broke out on my upper lip. I could totally feel it in my armpits. It was a good thing I'd put on extra deodorant for the airplane.

"So," she said, "my parents were saying you guys solve mysteries . . . ?"

"Yeah," Frank answered smoothly. He'd picked up from my wide eyes and desperate gaze that I probably wasn't going be the best conversationalist at the moment. "We've gotten into a tight situation or two."

We'd done a lot more than that. Back home, my brother and I were the ones to call if you had a case that needed solving, though admittedly, some folks hadn't always been thrilled about us poking around. Still, that was Frank. Proud of himself—of us—but humble.

"And Jacqueline tells us that *you're* a falconer," Dad said, jumping in.

"Sure am," Kate said, smiling, bright and blinding.

I blinked. "A what?"

"A falconer."

Had I heard her right? "A . . . a real live falconer? Like the ones you read about in fantasy books?"

"Sure," she said, shrugging. "Except falconry isn't fantasy to me. It's my real life. I've got my own bird, and she's the fastest one I've ever seen."

"Wow," I said.

She studied me for a moment. "Actually, I haven't taken her out today. If you guys want to come with me while I fly her, I guess that would be all right."

My jaw dropped. That sounded *awesome*. I jumped in before Frank could say anything to ruin the moment. "Yes. Yes! Wow, yes, absolutely."

Kate's eyes lit up. Frank slid a look at me. Maybe the enthusiasm had been . . . a little much.

"I mean, uh, yeah, sure. That would be okay."

Kate laughed. "Cool. We can head out after dinner."

Mom and Dad accompanied the elder Adenshaws into the kitchen, and a moment later, I heard the sounds of the opening and closing of cabinets followed by the sizzle of a frying pan. Frank and Kate followed. I was starving but was the last one to leave the living room. I was too busy catching my breath.

I didn't care if I *did* sound like Frank. Kate Adenshaw was gorgeous, funny, and an adventurer, like us—not to mention, she was a real live falconer.

Boy, was I in trouble.

RULES OF FLIGHT

2

FRANK

DINNER FELT LIKE IT TOOK A MILLION years. While I might not have been literally bouncing in my chair like my younger brother, falcon hunting sounded incredible, and I was excited to see Kate and her bird in action.

The parents offered to wash up while we headed out. When Joe and I went to grab our coats, Kate grinned and shook her head. For her, it was the warm season. I sheepishly put on my huge jacket before we headed out the door.

"Follow me," she said, jerking her head toward a little outbuilding in the trees.

I glanced over at Joe, whose eyes were big and round as he stared after her. The way he'd been gaping at her when we first got here, and then stuttering his way all through dinner,

I wasn't sure whether he was more excited to catch a glimpse of the falcon's housing or to be around Kate.

We waited outside the shedlike enclosure until Kate came back out with her bird.

"Oh, wow," I said, taking a step toward them to get a better look. It was eight o'clock, but still light out, so I didn't have trouble taking in every detail. Her falcon was small—a lot smaller than I'd expected. I guess I'd been imagining a huge hawk, something that could eat me, or at least my foot. But the bird perched on Kate's wrist was a little guy, not more than a foot long, maybe a couple pounds. He had silver wings and a white chest with speckles all over it. A bright yellow beak curved from his face, and piercing dark eyes seemed to be following my every movement, as if he were sizing me up, wondering whether or not he could take me.

"Don't touch," warned Kate, and I lifted my hands in the air and backed up a step.

The falcon's talons curved around Kate's wrist, which was encased in a huge brown glove that was thick and leathery and reached nearly to her elbow. I couldn't believe a wild bird like that would just sit there, so calm and still.

I noticed a small, ropelike cord attached to the falcon's leg, just above its foot, connecting the bird to Kate's glove. Still, it wasn't like he was trying to fly free. This falcon clearly trusted her.

Kate jerked her head toward the trees again, and Joe and I followed her as she made her way across the yard.

"What's his name?" Joe asked.

"*Her* name," Kate said pointedly, "is Steve."

Joe sputtered, "What?"

"What do you mean, 'what'? You've never met a Steve before?"

"I . . . well." Joe blinked and looked at me, as if to say *Help!* I shrugged, and we made our way into the Alaskan forest.

"This isn't a great place to hunt," Kate explained as we picked our way through the bracken, since there wasn't a clear path. The wood was thick and dense. Slippery moss covered the ground and dripped from the massive trees. The air felt wet, which only made me shiver more. The forest must have been ancient.

"Why not?" Joe asked. "I would think the trees would be a great place for her to perch while she's waiting."

"This area's just too cluttered and dense. It's hard for Steve to really do what she needs to do with all the trees so close together. Peregrines are built for speed. It's hard for them to see their prey in here, for one thing. And then to get up to the speeds they do when they hunt? Almost impossible." Kate flashed us a proud look. "That's not to say that Steve hasn't flown here and done it well. It's just not where she shines."

I nodded. "So then where do we—oh."

The swath of trees opened up into a huge clearing. It looked like something out of one of the fantasy books Joe had . . . intelligently . . . mentioned earlier. Wide-open space—grass and rock as far as I could see. In the distance, mountains peaked gray, sharp, and snow-capped, and somewhere beyond them was even more ocean. Beach and rock and inlets everywhere. It almost didn't feel real. I shut my eyes for a second, just to breathe in the salty, frosted air. Mountains and fields at our front and ocean at our back. No wonder Mom and Dad wanted to bring us here. I'd been a little bummed at first, to tell you the truth. Things were really going well with Charlene, and I'd been kind of reluctant to give up the first week of any kind of real warmth with her to hide away in the Arctic. But seeing all this now, I had to admit Alaska was *cool*.

And it was about to get cooler.

Kate signaled for us to stop, and I swear, I'd never seen Joe scramble so fast to follow directions. She whispered something to Steve. Running her hand over the bird's back, Kate eyed the horizon, then thrust her arm into the sky, and Steve kicked off.

"*Whoa,*" Joe and I said at the same time.

My brother and I had solved mysteries in haunted houses, swum with sharks, and faced showdowns on Revolutionary War battleships, but neither of us had ever watched a falcon hunt. I don't think I've ever seen something so wild.

"Did you raise her?" I asked, watching Steve soar.

"No," Kate said, stepping up beside me, her eyes on the sky. "That's not usually how falconry works."

"How *does* it work?" Joe asked.

"I apprenticed for about two years with this amazing falconer named Debra. She took me out and showed me how to care for the birds, how to fly them, how to catch one on my own. Then we went out together and caught my first bird—a red-tailed hawk. Wow, he was some bird. An eye like none I've ever met. That is, until Steve." Kate smiled, lost in her own thoughts for a moment. "Anyway, Debra showed me the ropes. I trained a couple of birds—none of them falcons like Steve. A couple of hawks. After that, I was able to set out on my own. I caught Steve around here a few months ago."

My brother snuck a glance at Kate before returning his focus to the sky. "So it's not like a lifetime thing? You don't keep your birds until they die?"

"Nah," she said, shaking her head and shoving her nongloved hand into her pocket. "You don't keep a bird like Steve for longer than a year or two. They're wild, Joe. You can't just trap them and keep them forever."

Joe nodded and the bird called out, piercing the quiet of the evening. It gave me goose bumps.

"How does one even go about something like that? Catching a falcon?" I asked.

Kate said, "I used a bal-chatri. You pop some bait in, and then it's kind of a cage situation. Doesn't hurt the birds. You definitely don't want them getting injured. Besides being cruel, it defeats the whole purpose of catching the bird in the first place, right?"

"Sure," I said.

"So, then," Kate said, "the real work starts. You slowly teach them to trust you and train them to your glove with treats, and—whoa, whoa. *Watch!*"

Kate crouched and raised her eyes to the horizon, and then I got it. What was happening in the sky required reverence. Steve had gone from quick flight into a dive, and if I'd thought the falcon was fast before, now she was the Flash. The dive was like nothing I'd ever seen. It looked like she was plummeting toward the earth.

Twenty feet from the ground.

Fifteen.

Ten.

Five.

I felt my heartbeat speed up. Steve wasn't showing any signs of slowing.

Joe let out a little yell. Not two inches from the ground, Steve yanked up and flew, just like that, belly nearly skimming the earth.

Kate sprang up and pumped her fist in the air, letting out a whoop.

"Oh my gosh," said Joe. "That's the coolest thing I've ever seen."

Kate smirked at him. "She got you, huh?"

"Nah," said Joe. "I knew she'd be fine all along."

"Whatever you say," Kate replied, her eyes twinkling. Joe looked the tiniest bit embarrassed being called out like that, but he was still grinning. We all were. A guy could get addicted to that kind of rush.

"She's incredible, isn't she?" said Kate after a moment. "I've never seen a peregrine falcon so fast. Ever. They've clocked peregrines at over two hundred forty miles per hour in a dive. Steve can do that for sure. She's special."

I could hear it in Kate's voice—how much she loved this bird. It was different from the way people usually talked about their pets. Steve was part of who Kate was.

"That's some bird," we heard to our left.

I jumped, and Joe screamed like a kid. He was still hopped up on adrenaline. At least, I was sure that's what he would tell me later. I decided to let him have it. Sometimes, you have to give your little brother a break.

Sometimes.

But though Joe and I had been caught off guard, Kate didn't so much as flinch.

"Leo," she said. You couldn't just see her scowling. You could hear it in her voice.

"The grace," the man continued, walking into the clearing and closing the space between us. "The speed. She's an unbelievable animal, Kate."

I didn't know why, but something about the guy made my hackles rise. He was smooth, probably in his forties. Fake tan, graying blond hair. Chunky, hand-knitted scarf. He was the kind of guy who wore a business suit out to a field in the middle of Alaska. He was even wearing cuff links. And he wasn't alone. Another man, shorter, with beady eyes and round wire glasses, followed on the slick man's heels. The toady was decked out too, but he didn't say much.

I looked between the new arrivals and Kate and narrowed my eyes, taking a few steps so that I was off to the side, but technically between them.

"Tell me something I don't know," Kate replied, squaring her shoulders as she turned to face him. Steve swooped from her place near the ground back to Kate's glove. Leo's gaze sharpened, eyes fixed on the bird.

"What are you planning on doing with him?" he asked.

Kate took in a deep breath, then exhaled through her nose. "*Her.* And you're looking at it."

Leo hooked a thumb into the pocket of his slacks and gazed up at the sky. Guys like that, they thrive on the power they get from forcing silence.

"I'm Frank Hardy," I said, just as he opened his mouth to speak. He blinked at me and his eyes flashed. I walked right toward him, hand held out before me.

He took it, giving it a single firm shake. "Leo," he said, glancing toward his compatriot when the man didn't respond. "Sidney?"

Sidney glanced at Leo, then nodded at me. "Sidney," he repeated. "Leo's assistant." I'd gathered as much. Oily guys like Leo always seemed to have mousy assistants they could push around. Helps with projecting power, I guess.

"Right," I said. "This is my brother, Joe."

"Hey," said Joe. Instead of stepping forward to offer his hand, he just stood there, glaring. I wasn't sure what Joe had picked up on, if there was anything to pick up on, but neither of us was being particularly friendly.

Leo focused his gaze back on Kate. He stood straight, spine rigid, face carefully arranged in a neutral expression, but the rhythmic tap of his finger on his pant leg gave him away. "It's just a shame," he said. "To have an animal like that and not run her."

"Some of us fly birds because we love it, Leo. Just what is it that you think I'm doing here?" she said. Defiance laced her tone.

"Playing with her," Leo replied. "She—"

"*Steve*," said Kate.

Leo blew out a quick, annoyed breath. "*Steve*," he mimicked, "should be racing. She could win millions. Don't you understand that?"

"I do."

Leo's composed calm slipped, just for a half second, as he let out a frustrated noise. "And?"

"And it's none of your business, California boy. You're on my land. Get off it."

He blinked, and his lips thinned into a smile. "As you wish," he said. "You really should consider my offer, Kate."

Kate practically growled once Leo and Sidney were no longer in view. She rereleased her falcon and stood there, fuming.

"Every few days," she finally said, breaking the tense silence. "That business guy from California thinks he owns everything, and that he can buy everything he doesn't. Leo races birds in this huge tournament over in the United Arab Emirates. He travels there every year, when he's not making huge oil deals and destroying people's—never mind. It's not worth getting into that now. It's a cool tournament, but it's not for me. Not at the moment, anyway. He's right about one thing, though. Steve is special. Leo's been harassing me, trying to buy Steve off me for weeks. Sidney always shows up hauling the stupid paperwork, ready to make the deal legal and irreversible the moment I agree."

I could see how upset Kate was, but Joe and I just stood there listening. I've learned from my cases that sometimes, that's what people need most.

"Thankfully," Kate continued, "that sleazeball leaves at the end of the week. He can go back home with his own mediocre bird and figure out how to make money off her."

Joe had moved closer to Kate—not threatening, just supportive and protective. Turns out, I kind of had too. Not that it looked like Kate needed any help on that front. Even so. The guy was a creep.

Kate held out her glove and Steve glided over and settled.

They locked eyes, and then Kate said, more to Steve than to us, "He's not getting her."

Not if we could do anything to help her with that.

GONE 3

JOE

THE SUN CAME UP AROUND SIX THIRTY a.m. Earlier than I'd normally like, but today was for adventure.

Frank was already up by the time I came downstairs in my jeans and coat. "Wanna explore?" I asked.

"Way ahead of you." He had a thermos of who knew what—coffee, maybe—and he was dressed in everything but his shoes.

The adults were out on the back porch, catching up. Frank pushed open the door to lay out plans with them and get clearance on borrowing a vehicle.

"No," I heard Ed saying. "We had to give up on the idea of getting a dog. Jacqueline's a tiny-dog person, and you

22

can't have 'em up here. Wolves will go right for them. Or eagles."

"Eagles?" said Dad. "You gotta be kidding me."

"He isn't," Jacqueline added.

I glanced up at the ceiling, imagining for a moment a giant eagle crashing right through the skylight. Anchorage was something else.

"Morning, boys," said Mom.

"Morning." I grabbed the orange juice they had on the table and poured a small glass. Lot of pulp—the correct choice.

"What are the big plans today?" asked Jacqueline.

Frank jumped in with, "There's some incredible hiking around here, right? I'd love to go out into the woods. Check out the beach and maybe some glaciers."

"Not glaciers," said Mom. "We've got a big glacier day planned as a family."

"Roger that. So beach and hiking this morning, though? That's a go?" I asked, taking a sip of my juice.

"Sure," Dad replied.

Ed got up from the table and came back with the keys to his truck. "You're not getting far without these." He flipped them around his finger and was just about to hand them to Frank when Jacqueline called out, "Wait!"

He arched an eyebrow.

"There's that big pipeline protest today. Kate and I were going to take the truck." Jacqueline looked at us. "If you're going to be out for only a few hours this morning, that should be fine, but if you wanted to make a day of it, you boys might have to try another day."

"Protest?" I said.

"Yes," I heard from behind me. I jumped and spun around. Kate was standing there in her pajama pants and a T-shirt. Her hair was still messy from sleep, but her eyes were sharp and focused. "There's a big pipeline going in, from Anchorage all the way down through Southeast Alaska, which means it runs right through, like, a billion tribes' lands, including Tlingit and Haida. Big-oil guys don't care about the damage it will do to the wildlife around here, or to us. They only care about the bottom line."

Ed smiled proudly. "Morning, baby girl."

Kate's eyes brightened, and she gave Ed a kiss on the cheek.

"So, yes, we're protesting today. You guys can come if you want." She flashed us a smile and waggled her eyebrows. "But this morning I'm running Steve. Wanna come?"

"*Yes!*" I shouted.

Everyone turned to looked at me, surprised.

"Y-yes. In a reasonable tone of voice."

Kate giggled, then left to get dressed.

She met us at the door with a smile plastered on her face and wearing boots that went up her calves. I wished I'd thought to bring better footwear with all the mud. Instead

I'd have to deal with tennis shoes and squelchy feet.

"You guys ready?" she asked.

"Yeah!" said Frank.

"I'm excited to see Steve in action again, but I'm gonna be starving by the time we're through," I said, going pink when my stomach preemptively let out a loud confirmation.

"Did you forget to eat breakfast?" Kate asked.

I had, yes. I'd been too stoked to see Steve again. "Well—" I started.

Kate sighed. "Run in and grab something if you want, but you gotta be quick about it. Steve's hungry too."

"Nah, I'll—I'll be all right. Don't worry about it."

"The parents are ordering pizza later," Kate said. "So I bet you'll live."

Kate must have mistaken my look of happiness for surprise. She rolled her eyes and said, "Oh, please. Don't tell me you're one of those guys who thinks we don't have pizza up here."

I laughed. "Is that—is that a thing?"

"Oh yes. I was at summer camp in Washington, DC, and a kid there asked me the exchange rate for Alaskan money. I'm not even kidding you. Dude, we use dollars! This is still America!"

Frank and I cackled, and we made the trek out to Steve's tiny bird condo in the woods.

"Be right back," Kate said before slipping inside.

We waited.

And waited.

And waited . . .

Rustling came from inside the structure. Frank and I exchanged a look. Something felt off.

Yesterday, this had been like a two-minute process, but it seemed like Kate and Steve were taking forever.

Silence fell in the trees. The wind whistled in the leaves, and the pine needles shivered.

I could hear Frank and me breathing; that was it.

It was spooky.

Kate broke the quiet, rummaging around, slow at first, and finally frantic. She was saying something. I couldn't make it out. Then I realized she was speaking in a language I didn't understand.

Something weird was happening, and I couldn't take it anymore.

I was this close to just going in there after her.

Kate finally appeared in the doorway, breathing hard, her face drained of color. She frantically scanned the horizon. "It's Steve," she said, shifting her haunted gaze from the trees to my eyes. "She's gone."

THE HUNT BEGINS

4

FRANK

"GONE? WHAT DO YOU MEAN?"

"I mean *gone*, Frank! She was here, and now she's not." Kate's eyes were wild, her face pink and panicked. I frowned and slid past her into the shed. Had Steve escaped? If so, maybe she'd come back. She and Kate appeared pretty bonded, and anyway, Kate always had food for her. From what little I knew about birds of prey, it seemed like their thought process was *eat eat eat eat eat!* If that was the case, Steve would probably be back after a night out, looking for an easy meal.

I crossed my arms over my chest. No, that couldn't be right. The cage was latched and not a single wire was cut or out of place. Plus, the shed door had been closed when we got here. Maybe the wind had blown it open, but it didn't seem likely—not when the cage had a locking mechanism that spanned both doors and latched them securely in place. I studied the little knob that slid into a slot, and when I reached out to try it, I had to use some real muscle to slide it free. I don't care how amazing Steve was—there was no way she was getting that open on her own. And neither was the wind. Especially not when the weather had barely even qualified as breezy over the last twelve hours.

No.

Which left only one logical conclusion. Someone had taken her.

I left Steve's structure and stepped back out into the woods.

Kate was a mess. She was pacing back and forth, muttering to herself furiously. Her hair was all stringy and staticky, probably from pulling at it.

"Kate," I said.

She didn't respond.

I stepped into her path and placed my hands on her biceps.

"*Kate.*"

She looked up at me and started crying.

"I don't know what to do," she said, wiping at her face. I wrapped my arms around her, and her tears soaked into my shirt. She pulled back and sniffled, gasping just a little bit. "Who could have done this?"

Joe, who had been standing back, circling the shed, glanced at me. He didn't look mad, but his face was screwed up in a funny way, like he was holding something back. Jealous, probably, that I'd stepped in here instead of him. I shifted back when he walked up beside Kate and set a hand on her shoulder. She turned her tear-red eyes on him like a lifeline. "I don't know yet, Kate. But we're going to find her. I promise."

After some discussion, we decided the best place to start asking around would be the falconry club, a gathering place for folks who raised birds and ran them like Kate did. I'd suggested reporting the theft to the police, but Kate had rolled her eyes at me and scoffed.

"Please, Frank. You think the local police are going to drop everything to help out a teenage Native girl? You've got another think coming."

This wasn't something I knew a whole lot about, so I didn't jump in. I just waited for her to explain.

"Like . . . I don't know. My cousin got her room broken into and a whole bunch of her stuff stolen—wallet, clothes, some handmade jewelry that had been in our family for decades. It took the cops a week to even answer her calls. By the time they deigned to show up, the perp was long gone. I doubt they even tried to find him. And honestly, that's pretty minor compared to all the stuff we have to deal with when it comes to law enforcement. They're not going to make me or my problems a priority." She sighed. "And even if that *weren't* an issue, no one is going to care about finding a lost wild animal. Not around here. We can't go to the police. They won't do anything for me."

"Okay," said Joe. "Point taken. Then it's up to us."

Kate gave Joe a suspicious look. "You guys want to help me? Are you sure?"

"Of course we're sure," I said.

"Why?"

"Because we're detectives. This is what we do."

I noticed Joe had stood up a little straighter and puffed out his chest. "Plus, you're a friend. We're not about to leave you hanging."

Kate was quiet for a moment, focused on the endless line of trees ahead. She gritted her teeth. "All right, then. Let's go."

We went back to the house first and quickly filled all the parents in on what was happening. Jacqueline wrapped Kate in her arms, running her hands over her hair, while Ed went to make some calls in the hopes that a neighbor had seen something. Dad went into full investigative mode, firing off a stream of questions the second Jacqueline let go of Kate and left the room.

In light of recent events, Jacqueline opted to skip the protest, so after a few minutes of interrogation, Kate grabbed the keys to the truck, and she, Joe, and I piled in.

Joe slid into the back, and I went for the front passenger seat, but Kate held her hands up. "Nope, not gonna be me."

I tilted my head.

She rubbed the back of her neck and shrugged sheepishly. "I kind of, uh, failed my driver's test?"

"For real?" said Joe.

She whirled around. "Yes, for real! I'm busy, okay? Between Steve and protesting this stupid pipeline, well . . . I've got things on my mind, and those things do not include parallel parking." She was grumbling a little as she climbed into the passenger's side. "I don't see why anyone *needs* to parallel park in a city this size. . . ."

So that settled that. I was this week's official driver.

The Anchorage Falconry Club met at the community center. They were holding an informal gathering at noon, and we made it just in time.

I don't know what I expected—a bunch of big, bearded guys in plaid and boots, or maybe long, flowing capes? It was hard to tell if falconry occupied the part of my brain that imagined rugged mountaineering or epic fantasy. Either way, that wasn't what I found. When we walked into room 21B, I saw a bunch of normal-looking people standing around chatting. There was some plaid, and there were some beards, but no one was sporting a flowing cape. In total, there were about twelve people, most of them dressed in jeans, T-shirts, and jackets, sipping lemonade or coffee and munching store-bought cookies.

There were no falcons or hawks flying around the room, and I don't know *why* I'd thought there would be. It wasn't like the local community center was going to jump at the chance to allow a regular event where birds dive-bombed visitors or left messes all over the carpet. All in all, the meeting was a lot less epic than what I'd dreamed up when I'd heard about the local falconry club, but that didn't matter. We weren't at the meeting for a thrill—we were there for information.

Everyone in the room seemed to know Kate. She was the youngest by a decade, and that seemed to make her something of a celebrity. For the most part, aside from polite nods and a few hellos, she ignored everyone and made a beeline for a woman in the corner who was about five foot ten, with dark, straight hair that fell to her shoulder blades. She was laughing, loud and big, with another woman—a short redhead in galoshes.

"Debra," said Kate.

The brunette turned and smiled even bigger. "Kate! I didn't know you were planning on making it today."

"I wasn't." Kate shrugged, looking down at her toes. It was really unsettling to hear the hopelessness in her voice. Even hanging out with her for less than a day, I already knew she was the *opposite* of that. Kate nodded back at us. "This is Frank and Joe Hardy. They're here helping me with . . . something. Something terrible."

Debra cocked her head, and the redheaded woman she'd been chatting with slipped away and joined another group of attendees.

"Frank and Joe," said Kate, "this is Debra. She's an officer of the club and basically my mentor. Falconry isn't something you can just look up on the internet and jump into. You have to get someone to train you—to help you out. I trust her more than anything. If anyone can help us with this, it's her."

Debra looked concerned and confused. "About what? What's wrong, Kate?" Her expression shifted slightly, moving from pure confusion to determined. Whatever it was, she was ready to defend Kate or help her, even though she didn't even know what we were here for. On the one hand, I respected that. On the other, well, if I've learned anything over the years, it's never to trust that just because someone seems safe, they are. Even if Kate trusted Debra completely, I needed to wait and form my own opinion.

"It's Steve," Kate explained. "She's gone."

"What?" Debra glanced around the room, then leaned in. "She's *gone*? Like, she flew off?"

"No," said Kate, shaking her head, tears springing to her eyes.

"You sure?" Debra asked gently, though she didn't seem nearly as upset as I would have expected.

"Pretty sure," Joe said, stepping in. "My brother and I kind of do this all the time. We're not detectives—well, not officially. But—"

"Oh, I've heard about you two," Debra interjected. "The Adenshaws have mentioned your cases to me a time or two."

I think I got about an inch taller with that, or it felt like it. Joe beamed, just as proud, but only for about half a second. It wasn't the proper time to get all hopped up on ego. We were here to help Kate figure out who would want to take Steve. Our biggest suspect at the moment was Leo. Maybe we'd get lucky, and someone would drop an important detail. Maybe he'd been hanging around, talking to members.

"It's pretty clear that she didn't just fly off," I explained. "You haven't heard anything about what might have happened?"

Debra narrowed her eyes. "No, I haven't heard a thing. But I'd be happy to help in whatever way I can." She put her arm around Kate's shoulders. "In fact, I insist."

Kate smiled and relaxed for the first time since we'd found Steve's cage empty.

"Have you noticed any folks paying extra attention to Kate or Steve lately? Or maybe looking to buy a bird?" I asked.

Debra thought for a moment, then shook her head. "No. But that doesn't mean there isn't someone. You guys don't— what you need to understand is that Kate's bird, Steve? She isn't just any bird. I've been falconing since I was a kid, and I've never seen anything like her. She's fast—*wow*, she's fast! And sharp. And dedicated. Steve might truly be the most trainable animal I've ever come across. She'd . . ."

Kate looked up at Debra, waiting for her to finish her statement.

"She'd what?" I prodded.

"Frankly?" Debra sighed. "That falcon would fetch a fortune in pro circles. Do you understand what kind of money you can make flying in real races with these birds? They hold yearly events all over the world. I'm talking six, seven figures."

"Yeah," I said. "Kate was telling us about that. Big market, huh?"

"Big in a manner of speaking," Debra explained. "There aren't a whole lot of falconers around. Falconry is more of a lifestyle. It's not like having a normal pet, like raising . . . iguanas or something. Still, the people involved in the falconry world can get *really* into it. Not me. I do it for love. But there are guys around who are deep in it for the money, for sure." I noticed she glanced at someone on the other side of the room—a guy in a baseball cap. I made a mental note to ask about him later.

"So you've never raced a bird, then?" asked Joe.

Debra shook her head. "Me? No. That's not my style. I just love the birds. The one I have now, Fancy? Wow, watching her work is a miracle."

Honestly, the more Debra talked, the more I trusted her.

"Listen," she said. "I know you boys don't know me from Adam, but you have to understand, I'd never hurt Kate. She's like a daughter to me. And I'd never touch her bird. If you want more proof, you can ask my spouse. I was with them all night, and then we were together at three a.m. this morning with Fancy, flying her. You're totally welcome to talk to them."

I nodded. We'd follow up with Debra's spouse, of course, but my suspicions had quieted.

"Hey!" Joe suddenly called to our left. We all turned to see who he was yelling at. A beady-eyed, short man wearing wire-rimmed glasses, and—

"Hey! Hey, stop right there. I want to talk to you."

My brother's determined and he has a heart of gold, but he's not always exactly subtle.

A murmur went up around the room, followed by some uneasy shuffling. The beady little man looked up. When he saw us, his eyes went wide.

I leaned in and murmured to Debra, "Do you know anything about that guy?"

She stared at him, suspicion falling over her face. "No. I can't say that I've seen him around here before." She frowned. "That's weird. I know everyone at this club. I wonder if—"

Joe started across the room. Leo's assistant, Sidney, was clearly headed out, and Joe wasn't going to lose him.

"I'm sorry, Debra," I said quickly. "It was nice meeting you. We'll have to continue this later."

Joe was already out the door, and I lit out of the room like a flash with Kate on my heels.

It looked like our thoughts about Leo's involvement were more than just a wild theory.

INTERROGATION 5

JOE

THAT RASCAL. ONE LOOK AT ME AND the little coward barreled out of the room. Pretty suspicious, if you asked me. Someone with nothing to hide wouldn't tear out of a quiet meeting like that. Not *that* fast. But I had to hand it to him—that guy could run.

I took off, nearly knocking over two older people standing near the door. I shouted out an apology over my shoulder. Frank would almost certainly take care of any damage I'd done. Meanwhile, I couldn't lose Sidney.

Flinging open the community center's front door, I sprinted outside, hanging a right when I heard frantic footsteps disappearing down a dirty, narrow alley.

I ran as hard as I could, muscles already burning. My

lungs were having none of it. It's harder to run in the cold! Slowly, I caught up. Sidney hooked into another alley, but this time I was right at his back. It didn't hurt that I'd had plenty of practice chasing down suspects.

"Stop right there!" I yelled.

Sidney whimpered but didn't let up.

With one final burst of speed, I'd have him. I reached out to grab his shirt, but just then he jerked forward. I almost fell to the pavement but quickly recovered. If anything, the near dive had given me the momentum I needed. I thrust ahead again, reaching out, and this time my hand found fabric.

"Hey!" I said, closing my fingers around Sidney's sleeve. "Stop! I need—to talk—to you." I would have liked to sound all cool and dangerous and threatening, but it's hard to sound like James Bond when you're struggling to catch your breath. Lucky for me, Sidney was exhausted too.

"Hey," he called out, looking me right in the eye. "I know you."

"Yeah, we've met. You and your boss. Where is he?"

Sidney blinked at me. "What?"

"Your boss. Tall guy? Broad shoulders? Takes trips to the woods in a business suit? Leo? Your boss."

Sidney pursed his lips, and I made mine look as snarly as I could.

"I just need to know where he is so I can talk to him, all right? And while we're at it, has he looked a little . . . I don't know, weighed down lately? Not exactly *light as a feather?*"

"I have no idea what you're talking about." Sidney straightened his spine and glanced down the alley. "Is that what you were chasing me about? You were looking for Leo? Well, he quite obviously isn't here. Now, if you don't mind, I'll be on my way."

It was then that I heard the rustling of little leaves on the road behind me, followed by a hulking shadow. "Looking for me?" a deep voice asked.

I tripped backward and whirled around as Sidney scampered behind the guy, and found I was staring up into the face of just the man I was looking for, only this really wasn't how I wanted to find him.

Leo slowly raised a dark blond eyebrow.

I cleared my throat and backed up another pace.

"Might I ask why you were harassing my associate? Or is this how you conduct all your friendly business?"

"Well . . ." I cleared my throat. Where were Frank and Kate? I took another step backward. "I wasn't harassing him. We were having an important conversation."

Leo smirked. "And, pray tell, what might the topic of that conversation have been?"

Finally, Frank and Kate came running.

Frank didn't stop level with Leo. He planted himself right between us. Sometimes I *really* loved my brother.

Leo eyed Frank, then shifted his focus to Kate. "Ah, yes. Now I recall where I know you boys from. Kate Adenshaw. Always a pleasure."

Kate's mouth was a grim line. "I wish I could say the same."

"Now, what can I do for you young people?" Leo asked. "I assume you weren't shaking down my assistant in a back alley for the thrill of it, hmm?"

I blew out a breath through my nose and stood a little straighter. Behind Leo, Sidney was taking his time brushing himself off, as though I'd really done damage. Please! He was wearing a ten-dollar T-shirt, just like I was, and there was barely even any brick dust on it.

I took a step forward, coming even with my brother, and squared my shoulders. "Mister . . ."

"Blackwell."

"Umm . . ." My mind went blank. He was so completely unruffled; it was kind of amazing. And I'd frozen in front of Kate, too. Not that I really cared about that. It just looked unprofessional.

Frank must have sensed my hesitation. "Mr. Blackwell," he interjected, smooth and confident, "can you tell us what you were doing last night after you left Kate's place, from around nine o'clock on?"

Leo's lips turned up at the corners as though he was faintly amused. "I'm sorry, but am I under investigation?"

Frank seemed annoyed. Of course Leo wasn't under investigation, and he knew it.

"Then what business of yours is it how I passed my time last night? Or at any other point, for that matter?"

I fought a huff. "Our friend here had something very important taken from her, and—"

"Steve?" Leo demanded, the color draining from his face as he shot an alarmed look at Kate.

Kate's lip twitched. "Please," she said. I noticed her stance was wide like a fighter's, and judging by the look on her face, I wouldn't have wanted to cross her. "Don't act like you don't know all about it, Leo."

The man's features settled into genuine confusion. "Forgive me," he said, "but I truly have no idea what you and your friends are talking about. You're telling me that your prize peregrine falcon has been taken? She's truly gone?" He looked up into the sky, as though he could find her if he just stared into the clouds hard enough.

Kate hesitated. The sincerity of the guy's tone was enough to make even *me* waver for a minute. Was it possible he really had nothing to do with this?

"*That's* what this was about?" Sidney chimed in. "You chased me through an alley and attacked me because of a *bird*?"

Leo set his hand firmly on Sidney's shoulder. "Hush. What the boy did was wrong"—he shot me a pointed look, and it took everything in me to remain standing there without trying to defend myself—"but you and I both know that Steve is more than just 'a bird.' She's remarkable."

"So you've told me," said Kate. "Like a hundred times. Am I honestly supposed to believe you had nothing to do with her going missing? Maybe after all this time, you finally realized you couldn't buy me off to get what you want, so you decided to take her."

Leo stifled a chuckle, but his eyes flashed. "Ms. Adenshaw, are you accusing me of the theft of that bird? Steve may be incredible, but all the falcons I keep are stunning. I've made no secret of the fact that I would love to get my hands on that animal, but if you three truly think that *I*, of all people, would stoop to theft . . . that I would take a bird from a child to secure a two-million-dollar prize . . . Well, I must say, I'm offended." He blinked at the ground. "This may be the most insulted I've ever been in my life."

Two—I'm sorry, did he just say two million *dollars?*

Frank and I exchanged a look. Kate and Debra had both told us that there was prize money associated with the race in the UAE, but that was an incredible reward. It certainly gave Leo Blackwell a serious motive. But he was so *sincere.*

I crossed my arms. "Just tell us where you were last night, Mr. Blackwell."

He did that incredulous non-laugh again and shook his head. For a second, I thought he wasn't going to say anything more.

"Very well. I'll play your silly game. Last night, after I left you boys and Ms. Adenshaw, I was having dinner at my hotel with a few of my business associates, and after that, had a late meeting with one in particular, who manages the Russian branch of my dealings. Sidney attended dinner with us. My associate, Mr. Rengler, stayed until around two in the morning. Sidney had retired for the evening, and after the discussion was through, I followed suit. Sidney and I are in the same suite for the remainder of our stay here, and he can vouch for my being in the hotel all night. As can Mr. Rengler, until two a.m. You may verify this information with hotel staff if you wish. Feel free to check suite seventy-three, rooms A and B." Leo reached into his pocket and pulled out Mr. Rengler's card. "Here is his contact information."

His eyes sparkled with self-satisfaction. It was a look I hated, but being a piece of work didn't make the guy guilty.

"Will that be all?" With that, Leo turned on his heel and ushered Sidney alongside him. As they exited the alley, Leo called back, "Ms. Adenshaw? Good luck with finding your pet."

Once the pair was out of earshot, I turned to Kate and Frank. "He didn't do it."

"No," Frank agreed. "I don't think he did either."

"I'd sure like to hit him in the face, though," said Kate, then flashed us both a sheepish smile.

I didn't blame her. After that encounter, I felt the same way.

"Well, great," said Frank after a moment. "We're stuck."

A DEAD END 6

FRANK

INNER THAT NIGHT WAS REALLY TENSE. Kate's head hung low, and she barely touched the salmon her mom had made, which was *incredible*. Of course it was. Everything around here was locally caught. Even the water was probably the best water I'd ever had. So for Kate not to be digging into food that tasted that good made the whole mess even worse in my mind.

"She'll turn up, Kate," Jacqueline said. "There's got to be an explanation."

Kate didn't answer.

"It's not unheard-of for birds to fly off like this," her dad said between bites. "Steve knows where she gets fed."

Kate snorted.

"This is a lovely dinner, by the way," Mom said, sensing the rising tension at the table. I can't say that it worked to cheer the mood in the room, though.

"It doesn't seem possible that she got out," I said, "but I don't know. Maybe it's worth checking again. Emotions were running pretty high—maybe . . . maybe we missed something."

Kate shot me a look of pure fury, like I'd betrayed her.

I threw my hands in the air. "I'm not saying she did! I just think we have to cover all our bases. Humor me. Is it possible that Steve got out?"

If she *had* managed to escape her enclosure, she could be anywhere now, off in the great Alaskan bush or half a mile away, hanging out in a neighbor's tree, or—

A storm rolled in out of nowhere, and the sky got so dark so suddenly it looked like someone out there had flipped a big, celestial light switch. And with the dark came the howling.

"Wolves," Ed explained.

The sound sent a shiver down my spine.

I wasn't going to say it, but if Steve had gotten out, *anything* could have happened to her. And I wasn't sure, but I bet falcons made tasty snacks for some creatures.

"Steve didn't escape," Kate said into her plate.

"We're not saying she did," our dad said. "It's a lead to consider, though. Is there anything out there that you can point to for sure to rule out—"

"*Steve didn't escape!*" Kate yelled, throwing her fork onto the plate. The clatter seemed to echo in the sudden silence of the dining room. Rain pounded on the roof.

"Kate," her mom said, a warning in her voice.

"She didn't! I *know* her, Mom. Steve's never tried to fly off. She—" Kate sniffed suddenly, and I fixed my gaze on my own plate. I'd feel rotten if my suggestion made her cry. "How is a falcon going to get out of that enclosure, huh? Her cage was totally secure. And even if she did escape it, how would she get out of the shed? Her fingers? Her opposable thumbs? It's impossible." Kate blinked down at her plate for a few more moments, then continued, "She's gone, and someone took her." She looked up, and she fixed her flinty gaze on me, then Joe. "And if no one here is going to take me seriously, I guess I'm going to have to figure out who on my own."

"Kate—" I said, but Joe's voice drowned mine out.

"We're taking you seriously. I swear. We do this for every case we work. If we didn't ask these kinds of questions, we *wouldn't* be doing our job. A good detective looks at every possible angle before deciding which route to follow. This process will give us the best chance of finding Steve."

Kate's frustration softened into sadness, and Joe reached across the table and set his hand on top of hers. I don't think he saw me raise my eyebrow, but it rose, whether I meant it to or not. I noticed Mom and Dad glancing at each other too. I doubt Joe saw that exchange either, but that was probably for the best.

"We're going to find her, Kate," he said. "I know I joke around a lot, but I'm serious when it comes to cases."

Kate looked right at him, eyes shining with hope, then her focus skipped down to their hands. There was an awkward moment as Joe realized what he'd done, before he snatched his hand back and went red all the way from his ears to his collar. "Well," he said. "Uh . . . I, uh . . . we should . . ."

I pretended to wipe my mouth, using my napkin to hide a grin. I was *definitely* not going to let him live this moment down.

Kate blew out a breath, then said, "Thanks. Both of you. I know. I know you're taking Steve's disappearance seriously and treating it like a real case. I'm just so tired. It's been . . . it's been a really long day."

Mr. and Mrs. Adenshaw looked crestfallen, but who could blame them? It was hard seeing someone you loved in this kind of pain.

Kate mumbled something, but it was so quiet, no one could hear her.

"What was that, sweetheart?" asked Ed.

"May I be excused?" she said again. "Please."

Jacqueline gave Kate a sad smile. "Of course." Kate was up, her plate and utensils rattling in the sink almost before her mom had gotten the words out. She disappeared, probably up to her room, and the table was quiet.

What was there to say?

It was Joe who finally broke the silence. He looked across

the table at me, locking my gaze with his. "We've gotta find that bird, Frank."

"I know, Joe. I know."

That night I couldn't sleep. The air was thick with worry—over Steve, and over how devastated Kate was going to be if we couldn't find her falcon. I tried to clear my mind, to focus on the steady tick of the clock in the guest room, on Joe's rhythmic snoring next to me, the soft warmth of the fluffy comforter around my chest. At one point, I even pulled out my phone, thinking about texting Charlene to distract myself, but that was a bust too. When I looked at the screen, I realized it was one a.m. my time, which meant it was five hers. I wanted to stay on her good side, and waking her up that early on break was not going to accomplish that.

So eventually, I guess I just gave over to letting my mind wander, sorting through what we'd found out since we learned Steve had disappeared. I wasn't ready to take Leo Blackwell off the suspect list quite yet. He *had* put up an impressive performance if he was the one responsible. Even so, it was time to consider possible reasons other people might have had for stealing Kate's bird. It might help direct our search.

Money was the obvious place to start. There are folks who would do practically anything for a shot at two million bucks, and that included stealing a pet from a teenager. But the only person we knew who entered that UAE tournament every year was Leo. Still, it was a lead worth examining more. Looking into anyone who was suddenly considering throwing their hat in the ring this year was a good call.

Or maybe someone wasn't interested in racing Steve themselves, but recognized the bird's value as a competitive animal and planned to sell her. Considering how eager Leo had been to buy Steve from Kate, I figured there had to be other buyers out there willing to shell out a pretty penny to up their odds.

Then there was the possibility that someone had just wanted to have a little fun. Maybe they thought Steve was a *really* amazing bird and they wanted her for the thrill of watching her hunt. Debra had said falconry was a lifetime of dedication, and though it seemed strange to me that someone might steal a bird to pursue their hobby, I doubted it would seem completely off base for someone who'd built their whole life around the sport.

Maybe some rogue scientist had heard about Steve's abilities and was so fascinated by her stellar speed that they'd stolen her to study. Or some extreme environmental activist had set her loose, believing wild animals should be free.

The possibilities spiderwebbed in my head, weaving and expanding.

I heaved a weary sigh. Lying here in bed, blinking up at the ceiling, wasn't getting me any closer to sleep. I rolled out of bed as quietly as I could, careful not to wake Joe. (As if that was gonna happen. Joe was snoring like a bear and hibernating like one too. Guess falling head over heels in the course of twenty-four hours really takes it out of you). I slipped on some jeans and a coat, socks and boots, and tromped out into the cold Alaska night. Maybe some fresh air would help.

Lucky for me, my cell had a killer flashlight, so I managed to avoid tripping over any stray roots or rocks. But even the glow didn't reduce the creep factor. The Alaska woods were the very definition of wild and untamed, and they looked entirely different at night. The trees loomed large and dark, and the wind whistled through the needles like a vengeful ghost. Who knew what lurked out there in the forest?

I took a deep breath. What I was planning was probably stupid.

But that didn't matter.

I was out here now, and I wasn't turning back until I'd at least taken a look at Steve's home again.

I approached the shed, shivering as I cast one more glance at the menacing woods. *You're just cold,* I told myself.

I tried the door. It took some real strength to get it open. I had to put my back into it, and I don't care how amazing Kate's falcon is—she isn't the Hulk. Even if Steve had somehow turned the knob, which didn't exactly seem likely, there was just no way she could have gotten this door open. I ran my light over the shed walls and didn't see any holes in the structure, though it would probably be worth triple-checking in the morning.

Once inside, I shone my flashlight into every nook and cranny. The building might have been a humble shed, but it wasn't a ramshackle one. The place was airtight.

Turning my attention to Steve's cage, I held up the flashlight on my phone to get a clear look. The cage seemed solid too. No wires appeared to have been chewed through. And—I froze.

Hello.

Inches from where I stood, there was a perfect footprint in the dirt of the floor. A huge one. Tomorrow I'd get Joe to come out and help me measure it. Just from looking at it, though, I was sure it had a size or two on me, which meant I was looking at a twelve or thirteen.

And beside it, I thought I spotted a few drops of blood.

I dropped to my knees. If I'd taken another step, I'd have obliterated the evidence. It was a wonder none of us had disrupted the marks when we checked out the shed this morning after Kate discovered that Steve was missing.

Holding up my flashlight, I tried to ignore the hairs standing up on the back of my neck when I heard the wolves begin to howl again.

Get it together, Hardy. Those wolves have got to be a mile off. Probably.

I was grateful I hadn't fled back to the house when I spotted one last bit of evidence—a piece of fabric, maybe an inch long, shredded. It was dark blue and yellow, with a print on it that was distinctive. Almost like a tartan or something.

My heart jumped into my throat and my pulse sped up. This was it! This was exactly what we needed to jump-start the investigation again.

I snapped a pic of the shoe print so we could take a look at the tread pattern later and try to, at the very least, match it to a brand. I gave one last quick look around the shed before tearing out of there, back to the safety of the Adenshaws' house.

I had to physically force myself to slow down as I approached the front yard, and I was very, *very* intentional about being quiet when I moved through the hall.

I should wait, I told myself. It was the middle of the night. No sense waking everyone up.

Still, I knocked on Kate's door.

Once, twice, three times.

By the fourth knock, she yanked the door open, looking very unhappy to be face-to-face with me in the middle of the night. "What?" she said. Her voice was flat, but I was so excited by what I'd found out in the shed, I couldn't even pretend to keep my cool.

I guess she picked up on that fact, because when I said, "Come with me," she followed without a question.

She padded behind me into the guest room, settling on my bed as I shook Joe awake.

"Wha-what?" he said, sitting up, his hair wild from his pillow, as he wiped drool off his face. His eyes shot open when he saw Kate sitting there quietly, and he threw me a look that said I was going to die for this later.

I didn't care.

"Guys," I said. "I found something. And it could change everything."

A MIDNIGHT MEETING

7

JOE

THANKFULLY, I KEPT A PACK OF GUM on the nightstand. Or rather, Frank kept a pack of gum on the nightstand, and I was within arm's reach of it. A guy gets woken up in the middle of the night, his breath just kind of smells like dirty socks. I chewed while Frank talked.

We were all sitting around in a circle on the floor. Kate dug an old notebook out of the recesses of the guest closet so we could write down anything important that sprang to mind. We made sure to keep the lights down too. We didn't want the parents barging in and ordering us back to bed. Time was of the essence in a kidnapping. Er, bird-napping.

"Steve didn't escape," Frank said.

"No, duh," said Kate. Her face shifted from excitement to

54

irritation. I couldn't blame her; this was not exactly a strong start.

"I know," Frank continued. "You've been saying that all along, and Joe and I wanted to believe you, but I had to at least check. And you're right. There's no way Steve got out of that pen."

Kate twirled a chewed-up pencil on the carpet. "Is that it? You woke me up to tell me what I already knew?"

Frank's mouth twitched. "No. I'm saying I found something. Look at this." He held out his phone. On the screen was a bunch of dirt, and—*oh.*

"Is that a shoe print?" I asked.

"Clear as day."

There was a funny little pattern in it. A lot of shoe companies did that so when people bought their product, they'd literally be dropping ads for the brand in the dirt with every step they took. This tread mark was distinct. It had what at first looked like little circles in a bunch of different sizes, but when you looked really close, you could see that there was something else there. "Are those—"

"Snails?" said Kate, scrunching up her nose.

"They look like snails," Frank agreed.

"Shells, at least. Okay, that's weird."

"I don't know. I think they're kind of cute," said Kate with a shrug. "Look, that one's so happy."

I leaned closer. I didn't really see it—it just looked like a snail to me—but hey, no harm looking on the sunny side.

"It's a big shoe print," Frank said. "At least a couple sizes larger than mine."

"So, probably a guy, then," I said.

"Probably."

I nodded, and Frank took his phone back.

"Anything else?" I asked. I was pretty sure that if all my brother had found was a shoe print, he would have waited until the morning to tell us.

"A little blood," Frank said.

Kate's eyes widened in alarm. "Blood?"

"A little. Just a couple of drops. And I think it probably came from whoever was wearing *this*."

Kate's shoulders dropped an inch as Frank reached into his pocket and pulled out a scrap of some sort of fabric. It was blue with little threads of red and yellow running through it—not quite plaid.

"Hey," said Kate, snatching the material right out of his hand. "I—I know this fabric. I recognize this pattern."

Frank's eyes lit up, and I leaned in real close. "You do?" I asked.

My brother was excited, though he would never admit it. "From where?"

"I . . . I can't . . ." Kate's gaze fell to the carpet, and she squeezed her hand into a fist. Then she shut her eyes and knocked herself in the forehead a few times. "Think, think, think." After a moment her eye snapped open. "Ugh, I can't remember. How can I not remember?"

I couldn't stop myself. Forget whatever grief Frank would give me about this later, I had to do something. I reached out and set one hand on Kate's shoulder and grabbed her wrist with the other. I couldn't watch her beat herself up over this anymore. "It's not your fault, Kate."

She snorted. "Yeah, okay."

"It's not."

"But if I can remember where I saw that pattern, we'll know who Steve's kidnapper is."

"Maybe," I said. "But we don't know that for sure. And it's not fair of you to put that kind of pressure on yourself."

Kate began to take deeper, slower breaths, calming herself down. Her eyes were shut again.

"If I can find it . . . if I . . . maybe if I'd been paying more attention . . ."

"But this is your property, and you didn't think some creep would trespass and try to kidnap your pet."

"Joe's right," said Frank, something that always made my chest puff a little. "You can't take this on yourself. It's the kidnapper's fault they took your bird, not yours."

Kate sniffed. She looked down, and I realized my hand was still on her wrist and the other was resting on her shoulder, where her hair brushed over it. I turned as red as a beet and drew back, nearly toppling over. *Great, Joe. Super smooth.*

What was with me lately?

I rubbed the back of my head. "Uh . . ."

Kate wasn't looking at me, but I noticed she was kind of blushing too.

I was going to get the ribbing of a lifetime from Frank later.

Snap out of it, Hardy! I took a moment to get myself together, then continued. "The point is, blaming yourself isn't going to help any of us find Steve."

She shook her head. Tears welled on her eyelashes. "I—you're right. I'm sorry, I just . . . I'm having a hard time."

"Kate," I said.

"Mm?"

I grabbed her hand again—I didn't care what Frank thought of it—and looked right into her eyes. "We are going to find Steve for you. I promise."

She sat with that for a second, then smiled. And yawned.

"But not tonight," Frank said with a grin.

"Not tonight," Kate agreed, stretching. Then Frank was yawning and so was I. It was three in the morning, after all.

"Thanks for waking me up," Kate said when she stood, turning back at the door. "See you in the morning."

I nodded. "Bright and early."

FOLLOWING FOOTPRINTS

8

FRANK

MOM, DAD, AND THE ADENSHAWS were planning on heading down to the sound to do some whale watching and a late lunch. They invited us to come, and I was game. Who passes up the opportunity to see *whales*? (Apparently, in Alaska sightings are pretty common. Lucky folks.) The parents were still cool about us going out looking for clues as long as we were back at the house by one p.m. for whales. We had the only vehicle; the deadline was firm. That gave us the morning to follow the clues I'd collected in the shed as far as we could.

Kate, Joe, and I met out on the front porch and hopped into the truck.

"All right," I said, as I pulled the car into gear. "So, what are we working with? Let's go over everything and come up with a plan."

"We've got a weird shoe print," replied Joe, ticking our clues off on his fingers.

"We've got that scrap of fabric," said Kate.

"And we've got some blood," I added, "but I don't think that's going to get us very far. Not unless you're best friends with a crime lab investigator, Kate."

"Nope," she said. "I know . . . a kid who's getting an A in biology."

That got a laugh out of me.

"Seems like the most logical place to start would be a shoe store," said Joe. "There are a few downtown, right?"

Kate shrugged. "Yeah, but what are you hoping to find out? That the thief wears Converse? So what?"

I sighed and made a turn toward Fourth Avenue in Anchorage. "First of all, that's not a Converse print. Converse sneakers have little stars on the sole." I wasn't exactly a style icon, but I had dated this girl, Jones, for a while, and she'd been crazy about those shoes. "Second of all . . ." Honestly, I didn't really know where to go from there. I knew figuring out the brand of the shoe print was pretty much grasping at straws, but with so few leads, at least it was something concrete. We'd take the rest from there.

"Second of all," Joe jumped in, "if we can find out what brand the shoe that made that print is, maybe that will lead us to another clue. If the shoe's a local brand, it stands to reason that our guy is probably local. If it's a big brand, like Nike or whatever—"

"I've never heard of Nike putting snails on the bottom of their shoes," said Kate.

"Point taken," said Joe. "As I was saying, if the shoe's from a bigger guy *like* Nike, it won't tell us as much. We're hoping for something small—maybe with a cult following. Make sense now?"

"Yeah," said Kate, reluctantly at first, but then she squared her shoulders and took a deep breath. It looked like she was ready for some investigating. "Okay. It still sounds like a long shot to me, but it's something."

"Yup," said Joe, as we pulled into a parking lot.

When we hopped out, I shivered. Even with the morning sun, the day was still pretty cold. We made our way into the first little shoe shop we could find and methodically went through, shoe by shoe, examining about a billion soles. None of the salespeople were particularly helpful, though a few of them really gave their best shot. None of the major brands had snails on them, and we checked *all* of them, then cross-referenced the available ones with lists of major shoe brands on the internet to be completely sure we weren't missing anything. Nike, Reebok, Adidas, Jordans . . . not a snail in sight. Kate found one local brand with starfish, but that was about as close as we got.

"See?" said Joe. "Now we know something!"

Kate scraped her teeth over her bottom lip and nodded, but said nothing.

She was right that the tread mark wasn't a major lead, but often finding the right answer is really about getting rid of all the possible *wrong* ones, so every wrong answer we knocked out could be bringing us one step closer to finding Steve.

"All right!" I said, infusing my voice with as much pep as I could manage. "One down."

Kate looked up into the sky, then furrowed her brow and locked her jaw. "And the rest of Anchorage to go."

Which meant we had no time to waste. If there was a snail on a single shoe in this entire city, we would find it.

But that was easier said than done. No snails at the first store. None at the second. And the third place would have been the longest of long shots anyway—all it carried were dance shoes. Joe shrugged and checked a few of them anyway. After six or seven stores, we were tired. By the tenth, it was impossible to tell which of us was the most deflated. We had *nothing* but a few Alaskan store owners who'd clearly thought we were nuts and a new appreciation for the art of shoe design. I'm sure there were more shoe stores in Anchorage, but this was getting us nowhere. I sat on a bench outside, dropped my head into my hands, and groaned.

"Well, this has been a total bust," said Joe.

"Not total," said Kate, smirking. "We know the kidnapper doesn't wear Nikes."

I raised an eyebrow at her. She half laughed and shrugged. At the very least, when we'd handed the print's measurements and the photo I'd taken to a ninety-year-old shoemaker, he'd confirmed that it was mostly likely around a size thirteen. And the shape of the heel, he'd said, along with the blocky print and rounded toe, indicated that it was most certainly a boot. After that, the man had gone into a long story about shoemaking back in Russia. Listening to his story had set us back a good twenty minutes. But it was *something*.

At the beginning of the day, I'd been fully prepared to go to every fabric store on the planet in search of a match for this mystery scrap in my pocket, but after our shoe hunt, that seemed like a stupid idea. Really, I should have known better. The fabric could have come from anywhere.

We were all exhausted and no closer to answers than we'd been when we first realized Steve was missing.

As we sat on a bench, gloomily considering our next move, Joe got out his phone and started scrolling.

"What are you doing?" I asked.

"Just seeing what I can find."

I peeked over his shoulder to catch a glimpse of his screen. He'd done a search for "snail shoes." Then "snail shoes Alaska," which only got him a bunch of Etsy shops that would do weird stuff like paint snails on canvas shoes. One charity shoe place even said they donated half their proceeds to a Save the Snails project. Kate and I hopped online too. While we were all tapping and scrolling, our faces buried in our screens, an old guy in a big coat and hat with a Santa Clause beard passed by and muttered, "Kids these days. Always on their phones. Don't know how to socialize anymore!"

After about twenty minutes of unsuccessful googling, we finally gave up. The internet was not going to save us. Another dead end.

We'd been sitting there in the cold for a while, quietly trying to think of any other detail to get us back on track, when Kate finally spoke up.

"How long do we have?"

"Before we have to get back to your house?" I checked my watch. "An hour."

She stared into the middle distance, then said with grim resolution, "I know where we have to go."

Kate had put the directions in her phone, and we'd wound up at a taxidermy shop. I'd wondered why she was so weirdly quiet on the ride over, but I'd figured it was that she was feeling discouraged by our lack of progress. It turned out her thoughts had gone down a much darker road.

"Kate," said Joe, his voice full of concern.

She stared stonily ahead. "I have to know," she finally said.

"I'm sure the kidnapper didn't sell Steve to a place like this." I was trying to sound reassuring. Apparently, it hadn't worked.

Kate whirled on me. "Are you? Because last time I checked, I was the one who said she was kidnapped. And I was right. I'm the one who knows her. I'm the one who knows this area and knows this sport, and I—" Her voice broke off and she looked down at her hands. "I have to know," she repeated quietly.

"Yeah," I said. "Doesn't matter how unlikely it is. We've got to check. You're—you're right."

We got out of the truck, one by one. Joe was the last out, and he shut the door quietly behind himself.

I doubted we'd find Steve here—I truly hoped that we wouldn't—but the anticipation was terrible. It felt like we were going to a funeral and ought to have been dressed in something more respectful than jeans, T-shirts, coats, and tennis shoes.

I pushed through the door and the little bell above it jingled. The space smelled like furs and chemicals. I took a moment to school my face, keeping it as neutral as possible. Joe was not as successful. His nose wrinkled, and I could tell he'd locked his jaw so he'd have to inhale as little as possible of the fumes. Kate, as usual, was steady as a rock. She was on a mission, even if what she found out might break her heart.

Taxidermized animals were everywhere—all sizes and kinds. Sharp teeth, big ears, winged, and otherwise. Creatures of the earth bordered the shop on the left, and those you'd find in the air were to the right. Joe tripped over a beaver on the floor and about fell on his face. When he got back to his feet, he was covered in sawdust. He slid a look at Kate, probably hoping she hadn't seen his lack of cool. From where

I was standing, I could see her mouth twitching and her eyes sparkling, but she managed to hold it together.

After a survey of the displays, I was pretty sure Steve wasn't here.

Gosh, I *hoped* she wasn't.

A man at the workbench stood up. He was a cheerful guy, at least. He had a wide smile that went almost to his ears, and his eyes disappeared when he turned it on us. He was tall and mustached—one of those old-timey, waxed ones that turned up at the ends—with eyes that twinkled. I may not have loved his line of work, but his face said you could trust him. If anything, that alone kind of put me on guard.

"Hey there, kids," the man said, his voice booming. "The name's Jed. What can I do ya for?"

He was wearing a navy-blue apron over his big belly, and he wiped his hand on it briefly before offering it to me.

I shook it, then opened my mouth to speak, but Kate beat me to it.

"My bird's gone missing," she said.

"Hmm," the man said. "One of mine?" He swept a look over his menagerie of taxidermized animals before turning back to us.

"No, at least I hope not," Kate said. "This bird was alive. She's my—my falcon. And what I was wondering was . . ." Up until now, Kate's shoulders had been squared, her chin up, as she looked Jed right in the eye, but before us, that resolve faltered. She blinked at the workshop's dirty floor, then her gaze rose to Jed again. "What I was wondering was if anyone had brought in a falcon to be stuffed recently."

Jed whistled low. "Let me make sure I understand. You think someone took your bird?"

"Steve," she said. "Yes."

"Kidnapped him?"

"Her," Kate said. "And yes. Steve is a peregrine falcon, and she's the most incredible bird I've ever had the honor of working with."

Jed ran a hand over his truly impressive mustache, then shook his head. "No, I can't say I've seen a falcon come in recently. And I'm glad to be able to say it. Truth be told, birds like that aren't worth much unless they're alive. I know there're folks around here who keep 'em and race 'em, but in my line of work, there's not a big consumer base clamoring for mounted peregrines."

I think every one of us felt the tension release from our shoulders. Steve wasn't here, and based on this info from Jed, she probably wasn't anywhere else like this either.

We thanked Jed for his time and headed out the door. I was glad for the fresh, clean air, but the sudden rush of it made me dizzy.

"Whew," Kate said. "I was absolutely terrified."

"Tell me about it," added Joe.

"What's going to be terrifying is if we don't get back home in time to make that whale-watching lunch. Mom will ground us for an eternity."

"She will," Joe said to Kate, his eyes big. "She's done it before."

Kate gave a tiny smile. Now that bird murder was pretty much off the table, we were all a little more relaxed.

We drove home and parked in front of the Adenshaws' house. While Joe and Kate headed inside to let the parents know we were back, I took a moment to make a few notes on the case.

I was just finishing up as they all flowed out of the house and piled, half into the truck and half into a car Jacqueline had borrowed from a generous friend of hers, so we could head out to whale watch.

As we cruised across Cook Inlet, coastal birds were lighting on the water, and when the whales breached, it took my breath away. You don't realize how massive something like that is until you see it up close.

But it was hard to focus.

All I could think about—all I suspected any of us could think about—was finding Steve and getting her back where she belonged.

FIRESIDE DECEPTIONS

9

JOE

WE DECIDED WE NEEDED TO HEAD BACK to the falconry club the next day. We'd spent most of the day sightseeing with the family, but it was evening now, and we'd been cut loose. After all the information we'd gathered around town yesterday, and learning at the taxidermist's shop that it was unlikely someone would have taken Steve for that reason, it made sense to go back to square one. It seemed that the guy we were looking for was probably a falconer, and more than likely a local one. Nothing was certain, of course, but in my experience, more often than not, the perp knows the victim, and the falconry club members knew Kate.

"I just don't like this," said Kate as she and I waited outside the house for Frank to finish up in the bathroom.

"Like what?"

She kicked a rock. "Suspecting these people. The people I love." She looked at me, her eyes dark and wide, shining with anger and hope. "The people at the club are my family, Joe."

"Yeah," I said. "I know. But—" I looked at the ground. I got it. Our first visit had been Frank and me doing our due diligence. But poking twice at people who cared about her? That probably felt like betrayal.

She locked her jaw. "But facing it head-on is still the right call. I know."

The sun was beginning to set, the sky painted in bright oranges and reds and pinks. With the gulls calling down by the shore and the cool bite to the air, under other circumstances I might have said the setting was kind of romantic. Kate's hair and face were lit up like a fire, and she was just so determined. So *passionate*. But I couldn't afford to let my thoughts wander in that direction. The last thing on Kate Adenshaw's mind at the moment was me.

Frank brushed past me and whispered, "Pick your tongue up off the floor, Joe. We've got work to do."

Thankfully, it wasn't so loud that Kate could hear. I would have hated to have a reason to add *kill my brother* and *bury the body* to the list of things I needed to take care of today. We were already on a time crunch.

Frank jumped into the driver's seat, and Kate and I hopped into the back. The falconry club was holding another meeting, and Kate expected it to be well-attended. She said the outdoor events, especially when they included hot cocoa competitions, usually drew lots of falconers. Unlike the first meeting we'd crashed, the night's event was invite-only, but Kate had already double-checked with Debra, who'd okayed us coming.

We rolled up to the woods' edge where everyone was parked, kicking up dust, and hopped out. For once, I was glad it was so chilly. It was perfect weather for a bonfire and cocoa.

"I'm gonna go do some asking around, see if I can get anyone to slip up," Frank said, before he headed off, leaving Kate and me standing awkwardly together. I could have sworn I saw Frank smile as he walked away.

The fire crackled and white smoke bled against the dark sky. I marveled at the stars smeared across the black as I shoved my hands in my pockets. "Is this what you get to look out at every night?"

Kate cocked her head and snagged a chili-pepper cocoa from a plastic table nearby. "What? You've never seen the night sky before, city boy?"

I rolled my eyes and grabbed my own cup, pouring myself a brew labeled *Chocolate-Covered Strawberry*, and I was totally here for it. "Of course I've seen the sky. Just not . . . like this."

Kate sidled up next to me, and I swear, my heart almost pounded right through my throat. "Yeah. It's pretty great. No one does it like we do in Alaska."

"You got that right."

"You know," she said, "Tlingits and Haida—the tribes I come from—are animists."

"Yeah?" I said.

"Yeah. We believe everything's got life running through it, one way or another. Even all the stuff up there in the sky."

"Maybe that's why your stars shine brighter," I said, resisting the urge to grin.

Kate paused, then shoved me with her shoulder. "That was smooth, Hardy."

I laughed, yet again going pink to my ears.

Kate downed her last swallow of chili cocoa, took another little Styrofoam cup, and filled it with a mix labeled *Midnight Black*. I was a little chicken to try something that sounded so bitter and intense, so I went with the white cocoa with orange and cayenne, which I quickly realized had been a big mistake. It was way spicier than I'd expected, and I wound up coughing until my eyes watered.

"You all right over there, Hardy?" Kate asked.

"Yup," I said, too loudly, my voice totally strangled. *"Fine! Super fine."*

"Let me try yours," she said, swiping my cup and taking a sip. "Oh, *wow*. This has a real shot at winning. Here. Try some of mine."

Suddenly my hands were all shaky and I was desperate to find Frank, but just as desperate for him not to show up to witness my sudden lack of cool. Trying to save face,

I downed some of Kate's drink. It was full and rich, but so thick it kind of stuck in my throat. Still . . . I liked it. It tasted like something you'd call sweet if you'd lived in the woods your whole life. Then I remembered I was drinking straight from her cup and she was drinking from mine, and I practically shoved her cup back at her. The liquid sloshed over the edges, making my hand all sticky, and I had to pretend I hadn't just gotten a first-degree burn on my knuckles.

"It's good," I mumbled.

"Mm-hmm," she said.

I rubbed my hand on the back of my neck. "Well," I said, coughing, because of . . . you know . . . the campfire smoke. "We can't let Frank do all the work, right?"

"Right," Kate said with a determined nod, but then she was coughing too. Seriously, what were they burning around here?

We wandered around, listening to little tidbits of conversation, tallying who was there. I had my eyes on the ground. There were a lot of folks in big boots here, and in case I was lucky enough to see that snail boot print in the dirt, it seemed like a good idea to check. Unfortunately, all the tread marks were just your standard fare.

It was nice to see Kate in her element with this crowd. She flitted from group to group, making small talk. Almost every conversation included some variation of, "Sorry to hear about your bird."

Still, no one seemed off and none of their answers struck

me as fishy. With no suspects in sight, I was about ready to pull my hair out, but to her credit, Kate was handling everything smoothly.

How's Penelope been lately? Oh gosh, injured? Weren't you planning on racing her? Oh, your daughter's moving you back down to the lower forty-eight and you're giving up falconry for good?

Been around town the last couple weeks? Oh, you were in Australia? Yeah, cool. Great. How were the . . . giant spiders?

No, no, I definitely want to hear about the run you and your ten children went on a few days ago—the specific day I just asked you about! Sure, I have time to chat about it. Of course I don't mind if it's a—a long story.

It was clear we were getting nowhere fast. The two biggest pieces of news in this crowd were (a) Steve, and (b) some hawk a girl named Ayla had captured, which was rumored to be able to hit near-peregrine speed in a dive.

Kate was talking to her right now.

"Yes," Ayla was saying, her deep brown eyes shining with pride. "I'd love to have you come see him sometime."

"For real?" Kate replied, and for once, it looked like she'd busted through the haze of losing her best friend. She was *thrilled*—bouncing on her toes. "I'd love that. Give me your number?" Kate leaned in close to Ayla, who was maybe a year or two older than us, closer to Frank's age. A few people were watching the exchange very closely, listening intently.

And then . . . "Hey, what if—I have an idea," I interrupted.

Kate raised an eyebrow.

"Don't let me keep you," Ayla said quickly, "but call me, and I'll let you watch us work." She winked, and Kate grinned in response before she ducked away with me.

News traveled fast around here, and it seemed to draw people in. Ayla hadn't had anyone come after her bird, but her catch was very recent. I wondered if she'd have any trouble tonight. We could call her in the morning and see, but maybe tonight we could rustle up a little trouble for ourselves. I leaned in so I could whisper my plan to Kate. "Worth a shot," she said after I was through.

Kate and I had decided to go for a Hail Mary.

If the bird-napper had been careless enough to leave a scrap of fabric and not sweep away his boot prints, if he'd been *that* sloppy, maybe we could bait him.

I leaned against a table where a bunch of people were standing around. "Well, okay, but this new guy can't be *that* fast, can he?"

Kate shrugged. "See for yourself. I'll show you."

"Yeah?"

"I thought Steve was remarkable," Kate insisted, "and she was, but this new little guy I snared yesterday? Wow. You won't believe it unless you see it with your own eyes."

I let my voice get a little louder. "Faster than Steve? I don't believe that for a second." We wanted everyone to hear—and maybe even start some rumors and spread the word. We figured we might be able to flush out the kidnapper if we gave them something they couldn't refuse. And how could you refuse an even better bird?

"Believe it. Not that I want to race him or anything," Kate continued, sounding a little bored. "You know I don't care about that kind of thing."

"Kind of a waste of potential, if you ask me," I said.

"I wouldn't call connecting with an animal a waste. Money isn't everything. Falconry isn't about the potential of winning millions for me." She really emphasized that *millions*.

"Wow," I said, still a little too loud. "I guess I'll have to come watch you run him tomorrow."

"You'll regret it if you don't."

From across the fire, Debra narrowed her eyes at us. She was probably wondering what the heck we were up to, and she wasn't wrong to be dubious. I knew we were grasping at straws with our little theatrical show, but time was running out, and every little gambit could be worth it. This could be the desperate move that forced a break in the case.

We took a moment to stand by the fire, sparks jumping. I was half-sick of cocoa by now, but I'd never tire of the smell of a campfire.

Pine needles crunched beside us on the dirt. "Sorry to hear about your bird, Kate," said a big man with a barrel chest. He was redheaded and bearded, with a handlebar mustache. I noticed he was wearing cowboy boots—not the kind of shoes we were looking for.

"Thanks, Gav," Kate said. "I really appreciate that."

I cocked my head and held out my hand, and he gave it a firm shake.

"This is Joe Hardy," she said, looking at me. "He's an old family friend. He's visiting us for the week, along with his parents and brother. And Joe, this is Gavin Heath. He's a falconer too. Well, of course he is if he's here. Anyway, he runs a red-tailed hawk, and he's incredible."

Gavin smiled, and when he did, his eyes sparkled. "Aw, he's nothing compared to Steve. I'm keeping an eye out for her," he said, suddenly serious. "The second I see anything like her, I'll get her back for you. No one deserves that bird like you do."

For a second, I could have sworn Kate teared up, but just as quickly, she blinked the emotion away. "Thank you," she whispered.

A nearly seven-foot-tall guy called across the fire, and Gavin walked off.

"He's a carpenter," Kate explained to me as we watched his retreating back. "He built most of the furniture in our house. He's been friends with my family for ages. Our families kind of . . . look out for each other, you know? Anyway, he's clean. I promise." She furrowed her brow. "Don't trust me on that. I think everyone here is perfect."

"Well," I said, "he's got the wrong boots, anyway."

"See? I knew that."

I snorted.

While we waited for Frank to circle back to us, Kate and

I watched the stars, alive or otherwise. The fire was a little too hot on my chest, air a little too cold on my back.

I was lost in thoughts about the case, even with Kate's arm no more than an inch from mine. I didn't know how to leave Alaska without finding out what had happened to Steve. It didn't feel like we'd just be failing if we couldn't figure this out—it felt like we'd be failing *her*. And I guess I could admit to myself that I didn't like that idea.

We drank in the silence for a minute, and then Kate laid her head on my shoulder.

It was nothing, not really.

Just her breathing, her hair tickling the back of my neck.

I about lost my balance.

It was after midnight when we trudged into the house, smelling of smoke. We were all exhausted, and yet, when I settled into bed, I could hardly shut my eyes. How was I supposed to relax? If I could stay up a little longer, maybe someone would come looking for Kate's mythical bird. Who knew? We'd laid it on pretty thick back at the meet-up. The bait had to have been tempting for someone there. If the culprit had been there at all.

This case had become so *personal* somewhere along the line.

Frank was out cold, snoring away, but there I was staring out the window at two a.m., up with the wolves. As the minutes ticked by, my certainty that I'd nab the culprit shifted to doubt and then disappointment. No one was coming. If they had, I sure hadn't seen them. I knew staying up wasn't doing any good, but now I was too tense to fall asleep.

I slipped out of our room and padded into the kitchen. Maybe the whole sick-of-cocoa thing had been a very temporary phase, because I was desperate for some.

"Oh!" I said, jumping.

"Joe? It's a little early for you, isn't it?" Dad was sitting at the kitchen table, a mug of coffee in front of him.

"I could say that for both of us."

He chuckled. "I couldn't sleep. The wolves woke me, and your mom is a terrible snorer."

I smirked and glanced down the hall. He was right—it sounded like a small bear was hibernating back there.

"What's got you up?" Dad asked. "Kate's bird?"

I opened the pantry door and scrounged around for some cocoa. Happily, the Adenshaws were total chocolate connoisseurs and had, like, twenty packets of the stuff. "Yeah," I said. "I just feel like we're missing something big. And it's not like we have forever, Dad. We might need to leave without figuring this out, and Kate could never see this bird again."

"You care about her," Dad said.

I sighed and waited for the microwave to beep. "Yeah," I finally said.

I avoided looking at him when I sat down at the table, taking a gulp before the cocoa had cooled off. Burn number two for the day.

"Well," said Dad, his voice clear and confident. He *did*

investigate for a living, and Frank and I were pretty well and truly stuck. "I think you need to consider a new angle."

I raised an eyebrow.

"Sometimes a person can get a little too close to a case," he continued. "You've been to that falconry club. You've been all around town. You've been in and out of that shed. There's something you're missing, and I'll bet you the contents of my wallet that it's right there in front of your face."

What Dad said made sense. The right answer was almost always the simplest.

"Who have you written off?" he asked. "Who's so wrapped up behind something else that you haven't thought of them in the context of taking Kate's bird?

I didn't have the answers, not tonight. But when I finished the cocoa and went back to bed, those were the questions that chased me into sleep.

A NEW LEAD 10

FRANK

OM, DAD, JOE, AND I HAD BROKEN off from the Adenshaws the next day and gone to see Portage Glacier. I was hoping that stepping away from the case for a little might give me and Joe some new perspective. The glacier was majestic and overwhelming. No one could possibly look at it without feeling tiny. As I took in this incredible natural site, I wondered how many more people would have a chance to see it before it melted and went away for good. I hoped that wouldn't happen anytime soon, but with climate change and the oceans warming, I couldn't help thinking about how little time we really had.

Part of me hadn't even wanted to go exploring today. I knew we were on vacation—our parents had reminded us repeatedly. We'd come to Alaska to spend some time together as a family and catch up with old friends. I knew how important all that was. But I couldn't get the case off my mind. Not when we were this deep in it.

Plus, something had gotten ahold of Joe. It was more than his crush on Kate. Lately, it was as though he'd been inspired. Of course, he always worked hard when he was on the clue trail, but this time was different. This case had gotten its hooks in him.

I couldn't bear to see Kate worried sick over her beloved bird, and I couldn't stand the idea of Joe failing on this case when he was so caught up in the outcome. It would really rock him if we didn't come out on top this time.

It was hard to focus on anything at all, other than finding Steve.

Maybe I just needed to get out on my own for a little while, clear my head.

I waited until all the adults had gone to bed. Dad had cleared me to use the truck; he understood the toll a high-stakes case could take on someone, and I think he recognized that I needed some space to think.

After grabbing the keys, I headed out. Mr. Adenshaw had told me to stay out of the woods at night, and I sure wasn't going to choose *that* bit of advice to ignore. There were bears and wolves and moose, who apparently were not like big deer and really could be dangerous. So, instead, I drove to the coast. It was empty at this time of the night, which was exactly what I needed. I loved being around people, but right then, what I wanted most was quiet.

I hopped out of the truck, taking a Coke and a blanket from the passenger seat. I scoped out a spot on a rock that overlooked the water and settled down to take in the view. It was moody and dark, especially in nighttime this black. I'd never seen a night sky so inky. But Alaska had a small enough ratio of people to wilderness that I guess light pollution wasn't nearly as big of a thing up here. The night felt real and vast and solid, almost like you could touch it if you wanted to bad enough.

And then, slowly at first, then all at once, the sky lit up green. It looked like space aliens were about to launch an attack on earth, and it was going to be a big one.

But it wasn't aliens.

It was the northern lights. I'd seen them in movies before, of course. But I'd never gotten to see them in real life. This was one of the most incredible things I'd ever laid eyes on. Lights striped their way across the entire dark sky, stars twinkling in between them. They were mostly bright green, but I waited, and they shifted, bleeding into purples and pinks. It felt so big and weird that a small part of me wanted to run. I didn't. I just stayed there, staring at the coolest sky I would ever behold. I'd come out here to be alone, but I wanted, suddenly, to share this with Charlene.

As the phone rang, I tried to come up with a slick greeting, something like, *Hey, so I was just looking at the northern lights, and the only thing prettier I could think of was you.*

I snorted at the cornball thought, and that's, of course, the exact moment she picked up.

"Well," she said, "Frank Hardy."

"Nope," I said, smiling instantly.

"There's this little thing known as caller ID."

"You reporters. All your tips and tricks. You can uncover anything."

She yawned before she laughed, and I realized what time it was in Bayport. Whoops.

"Sorry, I didn't mean to wake you up. Kind of forgot about the time difference."

"It's okay," she said. "I fell asleep at my laptop, anyway. It would have woken up with some crick in my neck if I slept at a desk all night. You did me a favor. What was so funny, by the way?"

"What?"

"When you called. You were absolutely snorting over something."

"Uh . . ." I scratched at my collarbone. "Nothing."

I could practically hear the grin in her voice. "Nothing? Must have totally invented the hyena laughter and snorting in my head, then. Weird."

"Just a . . . seal. Out here. On the beach."

"Mm-hmm," she said. "I'm sure."

"Please. Would I lie to you?" She was almost certainly rolling her eyes at that one. *Come on, Hardy!*

I stretched out, laying my head on one of my hands and pressing the phone to my ear with the other. "How are you?"

"Good," she said. "Busy. I'm working on a big story right now."

"Yeah? What's it about?"

"I can't tell you that!"

"Why not?"

Her voice went very prim and proper. "You can hear about it with everybody else in Bayport in four days."

"Fair enough. I'll be back in town by then."

"Good," she said. "How's the Arctic?"

"Well, guess what I'm looking at right now."

"Hmmm, besides the seal that definitely exists?"

"Besides the seal."

"A polar bear. I hope you're behind some sort of barrier."

I stared up at the sky. "The northern lights."

She paused for a beat. "No way."

"Yeah. It's one of the most amazing things I've ever seen. I can't believe everyone in the state isn't outside looking up at this right now."

"Well, I think if you live somewhere and you look at something often enough, it stops seeming so extraordinary and just becomes normal, you know?"

"Yeah, I guess."

There was quiet for a moment, before I said, "I just can't imagine how *this* could ever get old."

"Show me?"

"Hold on." I ruffled my hair a little. If she wanted to video-chat, I didn't want to look like a total dork. After a quick check using selfie mode on my phone, I switched to video mode and held up my phone to take in the view.

"Oh, *wow*," she said. "That really is amazing. Look at all those stars sparkling. It looks like someone spread glitter paint across the sky."

"Right? I wish you could see it with me from here. In person."

"Turn the camera so I can see you."

"One sec." It was a good thing I fixed my hair.

"I kind of thought you were exaggerating about the colors. Did you know most northern lights sightings are just green?"

"I did not."

"I did a deep dive for a story a couple years ago, when people could see them up and down the coast if they were in the right place at the right time."

I grinned. "You're a nerd."

"So are you." She shifted so she was lying on her stomach and laid her chin in her hand, hair falling around her shoulders. "So," she said, "what have you been up to in Anchorage? Besides looking at pretty lights in the sky and hanging out on moody beaches in the dark?"

There it was: right back to where I was before I'd driven out here. My brain snapped into overdrive. "Working a case."

"A case? Frank Hardy, you're supposed to be on vacation!"

"I know, I know. But we're staying with a family friend, and her bird got stolen."

"Wait, her what? You're going to have to back up for me."

I sighed and explained everything to Charlene—who Kate was, what falconry entailed, the fact that people still practiced the sport in the modern day. After that, I told her about how Steve had disappeared and that we were entirely stuck investigating what had happened to her and had less than forty-eight hours to figure it all out and save the day.

"Wow," she said. "So much for a relaxing week in the north."

"So, what do you think? Does the whole thing sound totally hopeless?"

"I don't know. Do you have any suspects?"

"Not good ones." I went down the list—Leo, Debra, Gavin—but there was a major reason why it was unlikely that each of them was involved.

When I explained that to Charlene, she was quiet for a moment, then said, "Go over the evidence with me again?"

"Okay, so in the shed, there was that speckling of blood. Then the shred of fabric, which we still haven't managed to match. The boot print with the snails in it—"

"Wait. Did you say snails?"

"Yeah, I know it's weird, but—"

"No, no. It's not that. It's just . . ." She ducked out of the frame for a second. When she came back, she was holding a pair of boots.

"Hey, I recognize those! You wore them when we did that space escape room." As soon as the words left my mouth, I regretted admitting that I recalled a detail that specific. But Charlene didn't even seem to notice. She was too excited.

She flipped the boots over so I could see the soles and—

"The snails!"

"The snails," she confirmed.

"I—where—how—"

"These shoes are literally called Snail." I immediately felt silly. But that brand hadn't popped up in my search. "They're my favorite," she continued. "My aunt brings me a pair every year because you can't order them online. Snail is *super* local, and part of their story is that they use traditional techniques and don't buy into modern promotional hype. They don't even have a website. That branding is why they have this cult following. All their transactions are done in-store, and I swear, they have a *fax machine* in there. My aunt said they just got a credit card machine last year."

My heart started racing. This was exactly the break we needed. "Charlene, do you know where they're located?"

"Atherton, California."

HOT ON THE TRAIL

11

JOE

KATE AND I WERE TAKING A BREAK FROM investigating. It had been a killer week, and we were all bone-tired. Kate had called Ayla after breakfast to check in on her hawk after word had spread about him at the falconry club event the night before, but Ayla had said everything was fine. At eleven a.m., Frank was still asleep, which wasn't a surprise, since he'd gone out last night and hadn't come back until after I'd passed out. Kate and I had stayed up playing video games (she wrecked me), so it must have been pretty late. Now it was just Kate and me at the beach. I loved spending time with my brother, but the current situation did not bum me out in the least.

Kate was gorgeous, and *relaxed* for once. The green in

her sweater made her dark brown eyes pop. She kept bumping me with her shoulder as we made our way down the coast. I'm sure I looked supercool when I tripped over a rock, nearly falling on my face. Thankfully, Kate caught me before I went down.

"Hey, Hardy," she said once I'd regained my footing. "Come look at this."

She was crouching near a tide pool, smiling from ear to ear. I knew a lot about tide pools, but I wanted to hear what she had to say.

"These are sea stars," she explained. "Everyone calls them starfish, but they're not really fish. Sea star is more accurate."

The one she'd found didn't have five legs—it had to have at least twenty. "Yeah, I recognize those guys. The bane of fishermen everywhere, right?"

"How'd you know that?"

"I live on the coast too, remember?"

"Right." She smiled as she poked around at the little snails and stars. I turned over a rock to see what lived on the bottom, but my hands got numb after only a few minutes. "You're into wildlife?" she asked.

"Yeah, sometimes. I'm okay with reading about animals and their environments, but what I really love is *experiencing* . . . everything. And what's more amazing than being out there in the moment, taking in the wild yourself?"

She was quiet when she said, "Cool," but it felt like more than a nothing-acknowledgment. I thought she meant it.

I hugged my jacket closer as the breeze kicked up and I got a face full of salty spray. "Oh, ugh!" I yelled, spitting and sputtering.

Kate looked up. Her nose wrinkled as she laughed at me. And she laughed long and loud.

My mouth curled a little at the corners. I guess it was pretty funny. "Watch it. I've got a whole ocean here to splash you with."

Kate raised a dark eyebrow. "You wouldn't."

"Why don't you come a little closer to the water and we'll find out?"

She laughed again, and I could feel it all the way in my stomach, and then—

"Joe! Kate! You're not gonna believe this."

Ugh. No, Frank. What are you doing?

That was what I thought.

What I said was, "Frank!"

He was breathless, sprinting over the rocks—red-faced and sweaty.

Kate and I exchanged a glance. Had he actually apprehended the criminal last night or something?

A huge smile split Frank's face. That is, until he tripped over the exact same rock I had. Birds of a feather, and all that.

He stood, slightly less cheerful about everything, and brushed himself off.

"Are you all right?" I called.

"I'll live." A few seconds later he reached where Kate and I were standing near the water's edge, then leaned over to brace his hands on his knees.

"Breathe, man," Kate commanded.

"Yeah," he said. "I . . . will. . . . I'm . . . fine. . . . Don't . . . worry . . . about . . . me." He took another second to gather himself, remembering how to inhale and exhale.

After it was clear that he was, in fact, going to live, I prodded, "Dude, what is it? What's so important?"

"Talked to Charlene last night."

I rolled my eyes. "Yeah? What else is new?"

"She knew about the shoes."

Kate's eyebrows jumped.

"Charlene recognized them," Frank said. "She *recognized them*. Don't you get it?"

"Not really, bro. The shoe lead was kind of a long shot when it came to ID'ing our guy, right?"

Frank shook his head. "No. I mean, yes. Yes, it could have been a false lead if the boots had been made by some major brand or even a brand with a website—with any online presence at all. But that's not the case here."

Kate and I looked at each other. My drawn-together brow now matched hers.

"Tell us," we said at the same time.

"The tread mark is from a super-niche brand called Snail. They're Charlene's favorite kind of boots. But get this—she can't buy them back in Bayport. They come from this tiny store. You can't even order a pair online, and most of their sales are done in cash. The store doesn't even have a website."

"Which means . . . ," Kate said, screwing up her face in concentration, "that the guy wearing them was probably local to that store."

"Bingo," said Frank. He could barely contain his excitement.

"Where's the shop?" I asked.

Frank said, "Atherton, California."

Kate settled on the closest rock. I tried to join her, but it stabbed me in the butt, so I relocated to the nearest *flat* rock while Frank found his own spot. For a few moments, we all sat there, birdcalls and the crash of the ocean the only soundtrack to our thoughts.

"Does anyone around here have a connection to California?" I finally asked, breaking the silence. Leo did. Of course he did. But the man had an alibi we couldn't get around.

"How would that help us?" Frank said. "Anchorage may not be huge, but it is a city. Visitors from California aren't going to be limited to just a few people we know."

"But people into falconry?" Kate said. "Those people, I do know."

"All of them?" Frank prodded.

Kate's gaze was fierce. "All of them. Definitely the ones close enough to me to know about Steve and know that she's worth stealing."

"It's often that way in kidnapping cases," I said.

Kate turned her gaze to focus on me then. "It's someone I know?"

"Maybe," I replied. "In the vast majority of cases we've worked, the person responsible isn't a stranger."

She shook her head. "That's the thing—everyone in the falconry club is local. Everyone except Leo."

Frank groaned. "This is totally maddening. It just keeps coming back to him, but he has an alibi."

"Yeah," I said, nodding. "But who else could it be? The facts are just adding up."

"Is there *anyone* else?" I asked.

Kate went still, fixing her gaze at some spot in the sea. "The oil deal," she whispered.

"The what?" I asked.

"The oil deal." For the second time today, someone was way too excited about information they intended for me to understand by osmosis. She literally grabbed my shoulders and shook me.

"Kate!" I yelled.

"Oh," she said, releasing me. "Sorry."

I gave my head a quick shake, trying to reset my thoughts. "Wait. The oil deal? The one you and your mom have been protesting?" I said when I was sure I wasn't going to fall over. "What does that have to do with Steve?"

I've never seen someone's face shift from thrilled to vicious so fast. Kate actually bared her teeth.

"The jerks from down south," she said.

The entire lower forty-eight plus Hawaii were down south, so that could have meant anywhere.

When I motioned that I'd need her to elaborate, she shook her head, locking her jaw, then explained, "I'm not sure where, exactly, but they run in the same circles as Leo. Most of them are from California, and, well . . . it's like this. This pipeline they want to build? The first plan had it running right through a wildlife reserve. That wasn't great. No one wants wildlife harmed, especially when a lot of the land is home to endangered species. The deal got national attention. A lot of folks protested, chained themselves to trees, that sort of thing. And with all the coverage, the activists got the pipeline rerouted."

"Wait," I said. "I thought—a few days ago, didn't you say it ran right through—"

"Our land. Yes. And a *lot* of it. It's not just Tlingit land, Haida land. It's the Athabascans, the Metis. More tribes too. But it doesn't matter which group owns the land. We're all *Native*. If you take land from one of us, you're taking it from all of us. They're running oil through it. What do you think happens when the pipeline breaks?"

"The Native communities are the ones to pay the consequences," said Frank.

"Yes. The pipeline breaks, and the oil flows right into the water supply. And who gets hurt?"

"Anyone on tribal land."

"Yup," she said.

"So why doesn't the company just move it again?" I asked. "Protesters got it moved for the animals."

"Please," said Kate. "You think that because folks around here made a stink to protect the native flora and fauna, they'd do it for the Native *people*? Not how it works, Hardy."

I looked over at Frank, who met my gaze, then toed a rock. "That's not right."

"Of course it's not right. But it is how it is." Kate crossed her arms over her chest and blew out a breath. "It's all about the money. Always is. Colonizers don't care who lived here first as long as they get to do whatever they want with the land now."

"I'm sorry," I said.

Kate didn't acknowledge my words. "They know as well as we do that water is life. They just don't care."

We all settled into an awkward silence.

After a while, Kate cleared her throat. "Anyway . . . Leo showed up here from California, along with a bunch of his friends. They've been in and out ever since."

I narrowed my eyes, remembering what my dad had told me the other night. *It's usually the simplest answer. Who is obvious, but in the wrong context?* "Yeah?"

"Yeah," she said. "A bunch of oil guys coming up, trying to finalize things on their big deal. Now, the pipeline—that's not something we can fix in a few days, all right? But what happened to Steve is. Leo's real buddy-buddy with a bunch of these guys in three-piece suits coming to profit off poisoning our land."

"Right," I said. "And he's so obsessed with your bird, trying to buy it off you over and over again. He goes back to his friends . . ."

"And he tells them all about how this local teenage girl won't see reason and make a deal," Frank said, picking up the thread. "He's frustrated about losing the opportunity. It's late and he's getting sleepy, so he tells his friends, who all only care about one thing—"

"Money," Kate said.

"Yes. He tells the businessmen the kind of cash they could make if they raced Steve in the UAE."

"Someone gets greedy," said Kate. "Maybe one of his businessman friends, maybe him, and he offers to split the prize with them if they figure out a way to get Steve for him."

"And then those guys take your bird," Frank finished.

"Hold on," I said. "If these oilmen are potentially in on the kidnapping, that busts Leo's alibi wide open. Aren't these the same people he was using to confirm his alibi that he was at the hotel the night Steve was stolen?"

"Oh," said Kate, eyes widening. "Yes. Yes, they are."

"He's not making it to that race," I said. "Not if we can help it."

THE DINNER PARTY

12

FRANK

WE DIDN'T KNOW EXACTLY WHEN Leo and his oil tycoon friends were heading out, but I jumped onto Google and found out that the big pipeline deal was set to be officially signed tonight, which meant it wasn't likely they were staying in town much longer than that. With us heading home in two days, the clock was ticking.

Now that we had a direction, we wanted to pursue it—pull an all-nighter if we needed to. But Mom, Dad, and the Adenshaws had made a good point when they tried to convince us to go out to dinner with them: we *did* have to eat. And Jacqueline was correct: brains didn't function optimally without calories to fuel them. We didn't have to be convinced *too* hard, even under the circumstances. We were teenage guys being offered food, and that's usually enough to delay anything, important or no.

We piled into the Adenshaws' truck and headed to the restaurant.

A lot of Anchorage was kind of coated in silt. That made sense in a city surrounded by mountains and wildlife and run by fishermen. People just tracked the stuff in everywhere, and what they didn't, Mother Nature did. But this place was *nice*. Not a dusty spot in sight.

We took our seats and ordered mountains of pasta and breadsticks.

Mom and Dad were talking to the Adenshaws about a scientific project that Jacqueline was involved in, and I was interested in listening to, until Joe kicked me under the table.

I frowned then mouthed, *What?*

Joe jerked his head, gesturing over my shoulder. Kate looked at me quizzically, but I just shrugged. I couldn't account for my brother's behavior half the time. He jerked his head again, widening his eyes until they were cartoonish.

I took the bait. Trying to be as inconspicuous as possible, I hazarded a quick glance over my shoulder. When I turned back, my eyes matched Joe's. We'd spent hours trying to figure out the best way to approach Leo again before he left town, and there he was, along with a bunch of men in suits.

I leaned across the table. "We have to go talk to them, right?"

Kate's eyes were shining bright, and her hand was clenched tight around her fork. "We have to. We're . . ." For a second, her eyes fluttered. "This could be our last chance."

Joe and I exchanged a look. Then I stood.

Dad looked at me, curious.

"I—we have to go speak to someone."

Dad pressed his lips together, just the slightest bit. "This is a family dinner."

"I know," I said, "but—"

"You've been out on your case for most of this vacation. I know what you're doing is important, but this is the last big family dinner before we go back home, and who knows how long it will be before we can make it back up here or see the Adenshaws again?"

"Dad," I said. "This is our final lead. And it's a good one. If we don't—if we don't pursue this, that's it. Steve could be gone for good."

The color had drained from Kate's face at the thought. We couldn't give up. Not when we were *this* close. Joe just looked at Dad with major puppy-dog eyes, and I had to admit—Joe had outstanding puppy-dog eyes.

Our father relented. "All right, but don't be too long. Your food will get cold."

Kate, Joe, and I set off across the restaurant.

"Leo," Joe said, pulling up a chair to an already full table, as usual jumping in headfirst before we'd even figured out what we were going to say.

Leo startled, blinking at me as though I had multiple heads. "Joe . . . Hardy, correct?"

"Yeah," he said. Kate and I stood behind him, neither of us trying to look friendly.

Leo spared each of us a glance, sitting very straight in his chair like he owned the place. For all I knew, he did. He gave a meaningful look to a man across the table. I couldn't quite interpret it. "These children"—I bristled at the word—"are acquaintances of mine. I believe I've told you about Ms. Adenshaw."

"The girl with the bird," said the suit to Leo's left.

I felt Kate stiffen beside me.

"That's me," she finally said, flashing a sarcastic grin.

I glanced at every man at the table. Someone here was going to give away something.

I hoped.

"Forgive me," said Leo. "I'm being rude. You know Sidney. And these are my associates, Robert, Richard, and Armand." Each of the men nodded in turn. Cordial and mechanical, like robots.

"I know who they are," said Kate sharply.

Leo, for once, was rendered momentarily speechless at the venom in her tone. He gaped at Kate, then understanding flooded his face. "Ah, right. I don't expect you're the biggest fan of—anyway. Have you found that falcon of yours yet?"

"I'm sure you know," she said.

Leo furrowed his brow for a moment before he managed to school his expression back to its usual superior disinterest. What did that look mean? I filed it away. Every word, every small reaction could be useful at this point.

"I'm not certain what you mean by that, Ms. Adenshaw. Forgive me."

Kate was practically vibrating with fury. "We still haven't found her."

"I'm sorry to hear that. She's a rare specimen."

"Yeah," said Kate. "She is. You've made it clear how much you admire the 'rare specimen' she is."

"Is this a purely social call," Leo asked, turning back to me, "or is there something I can do for you? We're in the middle of an important meeting."

I pretended to drop my phone. "Oh, sorry about that. Give me just a moment." I ducked quickly under the table. Of course, none of them was wearing boots. Each man was in a suit—at this point, I thought Leo might have *slept* in a three-piece. And suits didn't exactly go with boots. Ah well. It was worth a shot. Plus, at this point, we *knew* someone here was responsible for taking Steve. It had to be.

I retrieved my phone, then stood, brushing myself off. "I swear, sometimes this thing just leaps out of my hand like it has a mind of its own."

"Mm-hmm," said Leo, narrowing his eyes.

Joe jumped in. "So, this is everyone's first trip up north, yeah?"

"That's right," one of the others replied. I couldn't remember his name.

"And where are you visiting from?" Joe asked lightly.

"Most of us are based in California. Richard is here from New Jersey," one of the others responded.

I mentally crossed Richard off the list of potential suspects. *Good. One down.*

I slid a look to Kate. Her hands were clenched at her sides. "They're here from Cali to take our land and lay waste to it. What's ours is theirs, right?"

Sidney stood, hands planted on the table. "Now, that's uncalled for. I'll thank you to—"

Leo set his hand on his assistant's shoulder, and Sidney immediately quieted down, sinking into his chair. Leo turned his attention back to us. "If you're here to insult my business partners over the ethics of decisions related to economic development around Anchorage, I'll ask you to please leave us to eat our dinner. We've heard it all before."

"Yeah, I'll bet you have," snapped Kate. "You don't care about anything but lining your own pockets, especially when it's not *your* drinking water on the line. You can just go back to California in your plush little suit and your plush little high-rise apartment and . . ." She took a deep breath. "I'm sorry, I got . . . that's not what we're here about."

"Then what *are* you here about? My shrimp is getting cold." Leo's normally falsely friendly eyes had gone hard as flint. In my experience, powerful men do not often enjoy having their motives questioned.

"When exactly did you say you arrived in Anchorage?" Joe asked.

"I'm sorry. Is this an interrogation?"

"No," said Joe, "it's—"

"It's an investigation," I interrupted. "Look, you've said it a hundred times, Leo. Kate's bird is incredible, right? I think you care about that. I think you respect the bird, and I think you respect Kate."

Leo's expression softened.

"We're on a major deadline, and you and I may not see eye to eye, but I don't think you're the kind of person who's going to leave a kid high and dry if there's any way you can help, right?"

In fact, I couldn't be sure of that, but I didn't have any choice but to risk it.

Leo blew out a breath through his nose and took a sip of his water. "Proceed," he finally said.

"When did you say you arrived in town?" Joe tried again.

"About two weeks ago," muttered Kate. Of course she knew. These guys had been a thorn in her side for ages.

"Two weeks ago," one of the suits confirmed.

"And what have you been doing since?"

Deciding to humor us, they each ran through their basic schedules, where they'd been, and who they'd seen.

"The time I haven't spent negotiating, I've been on fishing boats," said one of the men.

"Really? Fishing?" his friend across the table asked.

"Sure. Not like I get in much time at home."

"Bet a big trip like this came as a relief," Joe said. "You get to vacation much in your line of work?"

The man nodded, and his glasses slid down his round nose. "Of course. I've been all over Europe."

"Yeah? Asia?"

"Once or twice."

"How did you like the Middle East?" Joe asked the question innocently enough, like he really was just making conversation.

"Never been," the man said. "And, truth be told, I don't have much of a desire to go. My body doesn't do well with heat."

"I fail to see how any of this is relevant," said Leo, tapping his fingers on the table.

"Sorry," I said, turning to face him. "My brother can get a little lost in conversation. You're right. We don't want to take up any more of your time than necessary. If you wouldn't mind walking us through your time here once again?"

"I've got my itinerary right here," Leo replied. "Would that satisfy your unusual curiosity?" He retrieved his phone and slid it across the table to me. I took out my own phone and snapped a picture of his screen. Leo didn't appear to mind.

By this point, Joe was leaning on the table, chatting with the man seated at the head. "What could a person do with a real windfall like that, right? I've never seen that kind of money in my life. I can't even imagine what that amount would look like all stacked up."

But even through Joe's multiple mentions of the race in the UAE, the country more generally, the hypothetical massive cash payout, no one gave so much as a *flicker* of emotion. This wasn't getting us anywhere.

Frustration bubbled in my gut. I couldn't remember the last time we'd been *this* close to solving a case and been unable to lock in the answer. It felt like it was right there, staring us in the face. If I could just—

"Where, specifically, did you say you were from again?" Joe asked, cocking his head. There was a glint of cunning triumph in his eyes.

"California and New Jersey," said Leo, beginning to lose his patience. "Are you going to continue repeating yourself, or—"

"No," said Joe, shaking his head. "Where in California and Jersey?"

They went down the line: Millburn, Los Angeles, Pasadena. Leo was sipping his drink again when the focus turned back to him. He waved dismissively at his assistant, who rolled his eyes and said, "We live in Atherton."

I had to fight to keep still and not let the excitement show on my face. I couldn't even look at Kate and Joe, but I hoped they were keeping similarly cool.

"Thank you," I said. "You've all been very helpful. We really appreciate it."

"Best of luck finding your bird," said one of the suits.

"Thanks," whispered Kate. Her voice was a little hoarse.

As we walked away from the table, I heard Leo say to Sidney, "Goodness, it's cold in here."

"It's always cold up here," one of his compatriots grumbled.

"Would you like me to retrieve your scarf from coat check?" the assistant asked.

"I lost it somewhere up here," Leo grumbled. "That was an *expensive* scarf. Handmade alpaca. I doubt I can replace it, and"—he sighed—"it doesn't matter."

Kate gripped Joe's forearm so tight, I thought she might break the bone. I could see Joe wince from here, but she sure didn't let up.

And pretty soon, I understood why.

"Joe," she whispered excitedly when we rejoined the parents at our table.

"Yeah?"

"The fabric. That shred that Frank found near Steve's cage?"

"Yes?" I said. "What about it?"

"I remember now. I remember where I recognized it from."

She shot a quick look back at the oil barons' table. "It's the exact same pattern as Leo's scarf."

OUT OF TIME

13

JOE

THE THREE OF US HAD STAYED UP late into the night talking through possibilities until we were all nodding off, and it was more than evident that it was time to call it a night. We'd woken up bleary-eyed but excited about our breakthrough. I *desperately* needed coffee. Dad humored me and I loaded it up with creamer, like I always did, and downed it.

Kate, Frank, and I sat around the kitchen table, dressed for the day, going over the facts yet again.

The difficult-to-escape shed meant that Steve had likely been taken, and the blood indicated that there had been some level of struggle.

The shoe print Frank had found had come from a men's

boot, and that boot had come from a local shop in Atherton, California—the exact town Leo was from.

The shred of fabric Frank had found on the scene matched a scarf Leo loved—one he'd claimed to have lost up here.

Leo also had motive. A lot of pretty decent people would do some less than decent things for a shot at two million, and if the oil deal Leo was pushing through said anything about his character (I thought it did), Leo was not "a pretty decent person."

"I don't get it!" I said, throwing my hands in the air. "All signs keep leading right back to Leo."

Frank frowned and stared into his coffee cup. Maybe the answers were magically in there somewhere.

I pursed my lips. It was so frustrating being this close to the answer but not quite getting it.

"Leo's got an airtight alibi, Joe," Frank finally said. "I just got off the phone with the hotel. I talked to them while you were pouring your coffee. Leo *authorized* them to speak with me, and that night, he was where he says he was." Frank slumped back in his seat. "I learned something else that throws a wrench into our investigation. We've gotta figure out what really happened to Steve. *We* might not be leaving until tomorrow, but Leo and his goons get on a boat this morning." Frank pulled up the pictures on his phone, then slid it across the table to where Kate and I were seated. "It's all there in Leo's itinerary."

For the first time since we'd found out about Steve's abduction, I felt truly hopeless. Maybe Kate really would never see her falcon again, and it felt like it would be all our fault.

I shook my head to reset my thoughts. No case was unsolvable.

Every mystery had an answer.

We just . . . couldn't see this one.

"It doesn't make sense. Every single sign says it's Leo," I whispered.

Kate dropped her head onto the table and groaned.

"If only he didn't have that alibi confirmed by multiple sources . . . So either Leo can be in two places at once, or he cloned himsel—" Frank frowned.

And then it hit me, too. "You don't think . . ."

A smile lit up my brother's face. "I *do* think."

As Frank jumped up from the table, Kate raised her head and looked at us like we'd both lost our minds. "What?"

"Come on!" I said, unable to keep the excitement out of my voice. "We'll explain on the way." I grabbed her by the hand and pulled her out of the kitchen on Frank's heels.

"Where are we going?" she shrieked.

Frank grabbed the keys and tore out of the front door. "The marina!"

In the truck, we filled Kate in on our mutual epiphany. Frank and I aren't twins, but sometimes we really do have twin brain.

"So," I explained, "this whole time, we've been thinking the person responsible for taking Steve had to have been Leo, right? If his alibi checked out, which it did, our entire theory of the case went up in smoke. But let me ask you this: How many kings did their own reconnaissance?"

Kate narrowed her eyes. "Joe, is this really the time for a history lesson?"

"Come on," I pleaded. "Humor me."

She shrugged. "None. They sent spies to do that kind of stuff. What king wants to spend time in the thick of it, risking his own skin?"

"Exactly," I said.

Frank stopped abruptly at a red light, sending us all jerking forward in our seats. (Thank goodness for seat belts!) What followed felt like the longest red light in the course of human history.

"Okay, but what do royal spies have to do with Leo or Steve?" asked Kate. "I'm not following."

"Powerful men send *other* people to do their dirty work," Frank explained.

Kate frowned. "Right, but we've already talked about this. We—" Then understanding washed over her face. "Oh," she said. "*Oh.* All this time . . . it wasn't Leo. It was *Sidney.*"

I nodded, glad we were all finally on the same page. "Once Leo saw Steve in action, he became fixated on having her. And then, when it became clear that you weren't going to sell, he decided he needed to find another approach—one that would make him getting his hands on your falcon a certainty. But does he do the deed? Of course not. No, he gets Sidney to do it for him. Guys like Leo always want to keep their hands clean. What a rat."

Kate was fidgeting in her seat. We were so, so close. "Can you go any faster?" she demanded.

"Not without breaking some serious traffic laws," Frank replied.

When he screeched into the marina, people had to practically dive out of our way. As Frank pulled into a parking spot, dust and gravel went flying. Something crunched and the truck shuddered. All three of us winced. *That . . . can't be good*, I thought. Still, we didn't have a moment to spare. The boat was leaving at ten a.m., and it was already 9:50. I hated even having to take the extra couple of seconds to unlatch my seat belt.

We all tumbled out of the truck and frantically searched the marina for a boat that was (a) the right size and (b) preparing for departure.

"Oh no," said Kate.

I could hear it—the monstrous sound of a huge vessel leaving port. The boat sliced through the water, groaning as it pulled away.

No! No, we couldn't get this close only to be five minutes too late.

"Wait," said Kate. "That's—that's not the boat we're looking for."

I almost fell to the ground in relief.

"Boats leave here only once a day to transport folks, and it's *never* before ten. That's a little cruise ship. For travel to the mainland, there's a particular kind of—yes, that's it. That's it! Let's go!" It was Kate's turn to pull me along, and if I got immediately kind of red and sweaty about it, well . . . I was running pretty fast, okay?

We barreled down the dock toward the boat, which was still boarding. I'd never been so relieved to see that a transport might be running late.

Or, at the very least, not running ahead of schedule.

And if Sidney and Leo were on that boat, so was Kate's falcon. Better yet, confronting the men on deck would mean that they wouldn't have a chance to flee. It's kind of hard to run when you're in the middle of the water.

"Little problem," I said. "How are we going to get on board? We don't have tickets."

"We don't have to get on the boat," Kate replied, pointing ahead. "Look."

There he was—Leo was thankfully pretty hard to miss. He was strutting along the dock, dressed to the nines, like he owned the place, even though he was surrounded by dockworkers and ocean brine and dirty sea vessels. I swear, his hair might actually have glimmered in the sun.

Frank and Kate both froze, but I took off running after our culprit.

Was it the smartest way to handle the situation? Probably not.

Was it efficient . . . ? Yes. Yes, it was.

I all-out sprinted along the dock, dodging people in my path. Leo didn't so much as look up until I was right on top of him. We made eye contact just as we collided, both of us tumbling to the ground.

"What in the world—" he sputtered. He grabbed me by the arms, and *whoa*, this guy had spent more than a little time at the gym. His fingers dug into my forearms, probably leaving bruises. I fought off wincing—I didn't want him to think he could intimidate me.

Leo stood, pulling me up with him. "What on *earth* is the meaning of this?" he said.

"You know exactly what this is about, you scheming thief," I growled. And I really did growl it—I was that angry.

"I'm getting to be quite tired of you," Leo said, shoving me away before leveling his icy glare at me. "Now, what are you babbling about?"

Frank sprinted up to us, Kate on his heels. "For Pete's sake!" he panted out. "Just drop the act, Leo. We've got you dead to rights and you know it."

He blinked. "What are you—Is this about the pipeline? Listen, young lady," he said, turning to Kate. "I know this is upsetting to you, and I understand that your community is shaken by it, but having your friends assault me on the docks isn't going to change the reality of the situation. This country runs on oil, and I've been assured that that the construction and maintenance will comply with the highest safety standards." He shook his head and glanced up at the sky, then met Kate's eyes. "I've got pockets deeper than you could imagine, and this pipeline deal is going to go through whether you and your neighbors like it or not. While I respect the gumption of all three of you, there's just nothing you—"

"It's *not* about the pipeline," Kate shouted. Her voice was trembling now. So were her fists. "It's about everything you're taking from me." She moved toward Leo, and for the first time since I'd met him, I saw a flash of vulnerability on his face. Something akin to fear. He'd rearranged his features, reassuming his haughty mask of privilege in a half second, but still I'd seen it.

I admired Kate. She was more powerful than she knew.

"I wish it was just the pipeline," she continued. "And I wish I believed I could do anything to stop your company's plans on my own, but my people have been dealing with selfish jerks like you for centuries, and in all that time, your brand of entitled hasn't been able to completely get rid of us yet. I'm going to do everything I can to stop this pipeline. *Everything.* But even if it goes through, we'll keep surviving. And you'll keep being nothing more than an empty man with nothing to care about more than himself."

If it was possible, Leo looked a little wounded. He pursed his lips, and his nostrils flared. "If it's not about the pipeline deal, then what *is* all this about?" he asked, quieter than before.

"Steve," Kate said, meeting his gaze.

Leo's face shifted again. "Seriously?"

"Seriously," said Frank. "We know what you've been doing to sidestep us. We know you have that bird, and you're not leaving with her."

"And what have I been doing?" Leo asked, an eyebrow raised.

"You've been using Sidney to do all your seedy work for you like the coward you are. We have all the evidence we need. Your motive. Your boot prints. Your scarf."

"My *scarf*?"

"Okay. Well, a shred of your scarf."

"I haven't seen that scarf in days. I went to bed one night, and when I woke up the next day, it had vanished."

That was not what I'd expected him to say.

Leo shook his head. "I'm telling you the truth. I'm sorry for your loss, Kate, and"—he turned to us—"you boys' dedication to your friend and her falcon is admirable, but I don't have her."

The puzzling thing was, it seemed like he was telling the truth.

"And," he continued, his lip curling, "I've never worn a pair of *boots* in my life."

Kate, Joe, and I all looked at one another.

And then my gaze landed on the man behind Leo. The little one with the big, round glasses who had come up behind us while we were having our exchange.

"You," I said.

Sidney caught my eye.

He froze.

He dropped the suitcase in his hand.

And he ran.

THE SHOWDOWN

14

T HIS TIME, IT WAS ME DOING THE CHASING.
Since Joe had tackled Leo, it was only fair that
when it came to stopping Sidney, I stepped up,
even if the person I was pursuing was probably
the easier target.

I heard Joe behind me calling to Kate to stay at the docks
and put all her energy into searching every inch of that boat
for Steve. Leo was flagging down a ship employee to get her
access.

My pounding footsteps drowned out Joe and Kate and
the rest of the noises of the marina—my footsteps and the
beating of my heart.

Sidney wasn't big—he wasn't even all that leggy—
but he was fast. He slammed his way through a couple of

dockworkers and some teenage girls strolling by the water-side. No one did anything to stop him. Just my luck.

Anchorage wasn't LA, the city of high-speed chases. And I guessed commotion on the dock wasn't really all that unusual either. I tore after Leo's assistant, desperate not to lose sight of him. If he disappeared now, we'd probably never catch him.

My feet thumped the pavement and sweat poured down my face. Sidney veered to the right, knocked into someone, spun, and was half a step from barreling to the ground, but caught himself an inch from the sidewalk. Regaining his footing, he made his way up the street, resuming his challenging pace. Still, his stumble had given me precious seconds. I was gaining on him. Sidney turned again, then once more, and until he found himself staring down a dirty little alley—just a few back doors to stores and a dead end.

He spared a glance at the filthy brick wall and the door behind him, then sprinted across the space, yanking at the handle. It didn't budge. Sidney ran his tongue over his teeth and looked at me.

"It's over," I said. "We know it was you."

"You don't know a thing."

"No?" I said. I took a step forward. "I know whose scarf the scrap I found at the crime scene came from. I know whose blood was in the shed." He hid his hand behind his back, but I'd bet a two-million-dollar racing prize that it had a nasty cut on it. I looked down at his boots. "And I know exactly what mom-and-pop shop you picked those up from. The soles just so happen to match the prints you left in the dirt of Steve's shed. You've got a boss forcing your hand and mountains of evidence stacked against you." Another step. Two. "So why don't you just give it up now?"

Sidney's gaze darted between me and the wall, as though he was calculating whether he'd be able to successfully climb it. Frankly, if he could scale that, he'd deserve to escape. When he locked eyes with me again, I no longer saw panic or desperation. Just anger. Determination.

He shifted, teeth clenched, and slipped his hand into his jacket. When he drew it out again, he was holding a knife.

I took a step back when it winked at me in the sun, but I didn't run. I couldn't. Leaving now would mean letting Sidney escape—letting him off the hook for taking Steve. I just couldn't do it.

I kept an eye on that knife, though.

Sidney's knuckles were white where he clutched the handle. I regained the advantage, closing the gap between us, careful to keep a decent distance between me and that blade. There was a wall of brick behind him and just a couple inches between us. For either of us to make a break for it, we'd have to get past the other, and I don't think either of us wanted to bet on who had quicker reflexes.

"Sidney . . . ," I said.

"Fine," he said through gritted teeth. "I did it. Is that what you wanted to hear? I took the little girl's stupid falcon. Seriously, all of this over a *bird*?"

I locked my jaw and took another step forward, but as I did, Sidney shifted his knife, and my stomach swooped.

Suddenly it occurred to me that I was utterly alone.

"Why?" I said, just to keep Sidney talking.

His eyebrows shot up. "Why? *Why?* Because I'm absolutely sick of playing second fiddle to Leo. You've seen how that man moves. Everything he's ever gotten fell right into his lap, and he's so—he's so arrogant. Why is he entering the tournament in the UAE again, anyhow? He doesn't need the money. But you know who does? You know who's overworked and underpaid and who *deserves* that two million dollars? *Me.* What's the little girl going to do with that bird, anyway? She has a contender—a falcon that could actually take the purse—and she's not even interested in competing. She just wants to play around with it like a pampered pet. Did you know that?"

I started to say yes, but as I opened my mouth, Sidney's fist tightened around the hilt of the knife and the blade flashed wickedly.

In the moment, I might have technically been the one keeping Sidney in the alley, but one wrong move, and I'd learn what it felt like to have a knife slipped between my ribs.

I clenched my fist in my pocket.

"She doesn't even *need* Steve. And as Leo *loves* going on about, that bird is an astonishing animal. Don't you understand what a waste of talent that is? If you think about it, I'm doing that falcon a favor. Doing everyone a favor, really. Don't act like you disagree. You know I'm right."

"You think it's a waste to fly a bird simply for the love of it? Is everything without a dollar value worthless to you?"

"Oh, come on," he snapped. "You and I both know—wait. What am I saying? You're just a kid. You don't know anything."

A muscle jumped in my jaw, but I took a deep breath to calm my rising temper. This was not the time to get riled up and do something stupid.

Sidney's eyes were wild, and he looked more and more like a cornered animal. "Well, let me give you some free advice, kid. You get older like me, you'll learn. Nothing in this life comes free, and the people who hold on to romantic notions like . . . like giving up their whole lives for a principle? Wasting every day, pouring all that time and all that money into playing with a bird they're never even going to see a cent from? You don't want to be one of those people. In the end, those people *lose*."

I scowled. Sidney's speech went against pretty much everything I believed in, but I couldn't tell him that. There would be no reasoning with him.

In the end, I decided not to say anything. There was nothing to say—nothing he'd be able to hear, anyway.

"Now, listen very carefully, kid. You're going to back away very slowly." He shifted the knife in his hand, and I flinched but tried to quickly regain my composure. I hoped Sidney couldn't see the sweat pouring down my forehead and stinging my eyes. He couldn't know I was scared—terrified. I gritted my teeth, focusing on not shaking.

A lot of good it did me. He shifted the knife. "Like I said, you're going to back out of here slowly and let me leave. Your little friend has found the bird in my cabin by now, I'm sure, and there's nothing I can do about that." The man's lip curled into an honest-to-goodness snarl. "But I'm not going down for this. I'm not."

I glanced over my shoulder.

I didn't see Joe or Leo or anyone. No one was coming.

My feet rooted me to the ground. I couldn't let myself get sliced to bits, but allowing Sidney to get away would mean he'd be walking the streets, free to take something from someone else or wreck someone else's livelihood for his own greed. The glint in his eye was so hungry. Who knows? Maybe he'd even come back for Steve.

I wanted to say something tough and intimidating, but it came out as, "I—" and died on the wind.

"Kid," Sidney said, "you've got five seconds to get out of my way, or I'm going to start getting mean." He glanced down at the knife in his hand, leaving no room for misinterpretation. He was tiny, but a lot tougher with a deadly weapon in his hand, and we both knew it.

Maybe I could tackle him? Catch him off guard? Based on the way he was holding that knife, he was no expert. One good hit to the wrist would send it flying. I was bigger than he was, and younger. I could take him down.

Or wind up with a knife in my gut.

The time was slipping away.

"One," Sidney said, taking a menacing step forward. I had a split second to react.

Flight packed up. Fight kicked in.

Stupid, I thought as I charged him. I was going to get myself killed. Adrenaline pushed me forward, and Sidney's eyes flashed wide as he readjusted his knife hold to one that wouldn't slash; it would pierce.

And then something thudded into him from behind.

The door! The door Sidney had tried a few moments before slammed open, right into the guy's head, knocking him to the ground, sending his knife clattering across the asphalt, where it came to rest close to my toes. Joe stood in the doorway.

I could barely breathe. My hands were shaking so hard, I couldn't get ahold of the knife. Thankfully, Leo did it for me.

He raced through the door right after Joe. This wasn't the first time my brother had gotten me out of a tight spot, and I was certain it wouldn't be the last.

"Frank," Joe said, coming to my side. "You're bleeding."

I frowned. "Am I?" I looked down, confused. At first I thought the blood was coming from my belly, but that was just my sleeve, brushing against it. Sidney had nicked my arm. "I'm fine," I said, flashing my brother a weak smile.

Sidney groaned from the ground. And then Leo hopped in and took charge of the situation. He shoved a knee in his assistant's—well, presumably, *former* assistant's—back and leaned down to growl into his ear. "How dare you? I've trusted you for all these years, and you went behind my back. You've sullied my name and reputation and you stole a pet from a *child*." Leo twisted Sidney's arm, and the assistant yelped. "What more have you taken from the people in my circle? From me?"

Leo turned away from Sidney for a moment and said to Joe, "Be a good boy and get me my phone, would you?"

Joe bristled, but he did as he was asked. Leo was helping us keep Sidney from trying anything until the police arrived, and with my injured arm and the adrenaline drop, the extra hands were appreciated. Leo couldn't hear his own hypocrisy, of course. That he was flaying a guy for stealing from a kid, when he was doing the exact same thing with the oil pipeline's impact on the water and land. Kate and her parents would fight it all they could. But that didn't absolve the man of responsibility for his actions.

"Suzette?" he said once Joe had passed the phone to him. "Be a dear. Please do a thorough review of my accounts. I'll need a detailed report when I get back to the office. And I'd like an investigation run specifically on my accounts that were accessible by Sidney Irving."

Even with half his face pressed into the asphalt, I could see Sidney go pale.

Sirens sounded in the distance.

"Joe?" I said.

"Got 'em on the phone while we were chasing after you."

I smiled. "Of course you did."

Joe rolled his eyes, and I pulled him in for a hug. I'd come this close to death just a few moments before, and if there was one person on this planet I was grateful for, it was Joe Hardy.

HEADING HOME

15

JOE

IT WAS OUR LAST NIGHT IN ALASKA. WE WERE hanging out by a campfire outside, even though it hadn't really gotten dark yet. I don't know that I'd ever get used to the movement of the sun up here, but it didn't seem to bug anyone else. If I lived here, it would be a bizarre adjustment.

We were roasting marshmallows—I liked mine golden brown, but I'd been surprised to learn that Kate liked hers totally charred.

"You're gonna eat that?" I asked.

She narrowed her eyes and took a giant chomp.

"But it's nothing but charcoal at this point!"

Kate eyed the marshmallow thoughtfully, and then she grabbed another from the bag, split it in half, and threw it at my face. Frank did a spit take when it hit me square between the eyes. It didn't fall right away—that was the clincher. It just stuck there, taunting me.

Kate giggled as she stuck another marshmallow on her stick.

I wiped the goo away and leaned back on the log I was sharing with Frank. Our parents chatted quietly on the other side of the fire.

We'd been able to keep Sidney on the ground until the police arrived and took him away. Unfortunately, Leo had missed his boat back home, but none of us felt all that bad for him. Turns out there was strong suspicion that Sidney was embezzling from him and had been for a while. While none of us left on terms that I would call friendly—Leo was a real piece of work, no matter how you sliced it—he at least seemed grateful for what Frank, Kate, and I had done for him.

But, more importantly, Kate and Steve were back together.

I hadn't seen Kate this relaxed since we'd arrived in Alaska. She was laughing and messing around. Her shoulders weren't permanently plastered up by her ears, and she didn't seem constantly on the verge of tears.

Earlier today, after we'd brought Steve back to her home, I was so exhausted that I'd flopped face-first into bed. Frank wasn't far behind me.

Not Kate, though. She took Steve and checked to make sure she hadn't been hurt (she hadn't), was otherwise in good condition (she was), got her happy and fed, and then disappeared with her into the wilderness. Kate hadn't come back to the house until maybe an hour ago.

I looked over at Frank, who was on his phone, probably texting Charlene. After the week we'd had, I didn't really resent him wanting to spend time with her. This trip had let me spend some real time with my brother, even if it wasn't the way we'd planned, and I was certain of one thing—I wasn't about to be replaced.

As the sun dipped below the horizon, the parents decided to turn in and leave us teens to our own devices. Frank was not subtle *at all* when he yawned dramatically, stretching his arms over his head, then told us he was going to bed early. I knew exactly what he was doing. And I was kind of grateful.

I could pretend all I wanted, but Kate was probably the coolest girl I'd ever met, and while I was looking forward to going home and sleeping in my own bed, I was sad that meant leaving her behind.

Part of me didn't think it was worthwhile to say or do anything to let her know how I felt about her. It might be better to just leave everything as it was. I could follow Frank inside, where he'd never let me live down how I'd blown my chance. . . .

But then Kate looked over at me out of the corner of her dark eye and said, "Hey, Hardy. I wanna show you something."

And with that, there was no way I was going back inside.

I followed her out to the shore, right near where we'd looked at tide pools together just the day before. Standing beside her, I shivered. Though I told myself the temperature was dropping now that the sun had finally gone down, I knew that wasn't the whole truth.

"You big baby," she said, laughing.

I shoved her. "Shut up! It's cold."

"Oh, for goodness' sake, *here*," she said, shrugging out of her jacket and shoving it at me.

"Absolutely not. I am *not* taking your jacket."

She rolled her eyes and groaned. "Just take it. I won't tell."

She sat on a rock—one big enough for both of us. After a moment, I lowered myself beside her. The water was so dark it looked bottomless as waves gently lapped at the rocky shore. Who knew what mysteries lay beneath the surface?

"Look," she said. "They're starting."

I glanced up from the water to the sky where she was pointing. At first I didn't see anything unusual apart from all those stars, which were amazing enough. Then a bright green slash started to peek through the black until it had taken over the entire sky.

"Holy crow," I said. "Frank was right. It *does* look like aliens invading."

Kate wrinkled her nose. "Is that what he said?"

"Yeah. I was pretty jealous that he'd gotten to see something so cool."

"I know," she said.

I smiled, taking in the ocean and the unbelievable sky. It was one of the most mesmerizing things I'd ever seen.

"So, are you still?" she said. I turned to face her and was pretty sure she was closer than she'd been before.

"Am I still what?"

"Jealous?"

"Of Frank? Nah."

We slipped back into a companionable silence, but this time I knew she'd scooted closer. I could feel it. A breeze blew a few strands of her long black hair, brushing them against my cheek. I studiously ignored it.

"I really appreciate what you and your brother did for me," she whispered after a moment.

"It was nothing. We couldn't just let you lose Steve. She's important to you."

"Joe, it wasn't nothing."

I shrugged. "It was right, then."

"Yeah," she said. "Even so, you spent your whole vacation helping me. And this is—Steve is the most important thing in the world to me. You both gave up your entire trip, and *you* . . ."

I looked at her then. My eyes were wider than I wanted them to be, I'm sure.

"You seemed to care so much. I mean . . . for you, it felt like it was personal, and you weren't going to rest until . . . I don't know if anyone has ever done something like that for me."

I looked back out at the water, taking deep, shaky breaths. Kate laid her head on my shoulder and I went stiff as a statue.

She smelled really nice, like the campfire. I forced myself to inhale, and made a decision.

Slowly, I moved my hand across the rock until I found her fingers. I swallowed hard, trying to force my rocketing pulse to calm down, before I slid my fingers on top of hers.

She laced them between mine, and for the next hour, we watched the northern lights play their eerie light on the sea.

Our flight was really early the next morning. It was still dark when Frank and I got up. We'd already packed, which meant I was able to squeeze in about fourteen seconds of sleep. It was a good thing too. Kate and I had stayed out on that rock for a long time last night, not that I had any regrets.

The Adenshaws were asleep, which we knew they would be. Apparently, even though the adults had turned in early, they'd stayed up all night talking with each other like teenagers until about a half hour ago. Dad never could sleep on planes, so he was in for a long day.

Mr. Adenshaw's truck was in the shop after Frank's reckless driving yesterday (oops). The damage hadn't been major. Our parents had offered to foot the bill, but the Adenshaws had refused after what we'd done for Kate.

The cab to the airport was scheduled to arrive at five thirty a.m. When it pulled up, and we loaded our stuff, I took my time, much to the annoyance of the driver. I guess I was hoping that if I lingered long enough, Kate might come out to say goodbye.

My family had piled into the cab, and I was opening the back door to get in just as pink and red started to streak across the sky.

I heard the screen door open.

"Wait!" Kate called. She was still in her pajamas, her hair a sleep-tousled mess, but she looked beautiful, all the same.

As I met her at the door, she threw her arms around my neck, then she whispered in my ear, "I'm glad I met you, Joe Hardy," before kissing me on the cheek. I could feel my face, ears, and neck burning red.

"Yeah," was all I could manage to get out.

She flashed me one last smile before slipping back inside.

I stood there for a moment, dazed, then slowly walked back to the cab.

It was suspiciously quiet.

As we pulled away from the house, Frank turned to me to say something, but I held up a hand. "Not a word."

The airport was dead empty when we got there. My guess was that not a lot of people fly out of Anchorage at any time of day, but especially not so early in the morning. Security was a breeze, and so was baggage. Pretty soon we were boarding the plane. Goodbye, Alaska. Hello, Bayport.

There were a few passengers here and there, but for the most part, we had our pick of the plane. Frank and I sat together anyway, me in the window seat, him in the aisle.

"Well, I'd say we had a successful trip," I said after the flight attendant had run through the usual preflight safety routine.

"I'd say you sure did," said Frank. His eyes were sparkling.

"Shut up," I grumbled, and we both laughed.

"Even if this ended up not being the vacation we expected, I'm happy it worked out the way it did. I'd say the next trip won't be so stressful, but, truthfully, I wouldn't have it any other way."

"Neither would I," I said, grinning.

I closed my eyes as we rolled down the runway and took off, my stomach swooping as we ascended.

We weren't all that high yet when I looked out the window to take in the forest below us, and I saw a bird soaring over the trees. It was small and fast, and—

"Hey," said Frank, leaning over me. "Do you think that's Steve?"

I hoped it was.